I0607592

Demon Daddy

THE BLOOD DEMON'S COLLAR

KD ELLIS

The Blood Demon's Collar
ISBN # 978-1-80250-588-7
©Copyright KD Ellis 2024
Cover Art by Kelly Martin ©Copyright January 2024
Interior text design by Claire Siemaszkiewicz
Pride Publishing

THE BLOOD DEMON'S COLLAR

Dedication

To the Data Sluts Anonymous
You know who you are!
For being amazing friends.

Chapter One

Pet

"Enjoy your last few days of life. It ends on the solstice."

The old wix's voice rattles around my brain like a pinball, making it hard to think. *The solstice?* I whimper as I realize it's only three days away, on the first night of Goddess Moon's visit.

"Oh, stop your whining. It's not like your miserable existence is worth much, anyway. You should be thanking me." The old wix grabs for me, and I flinch back, but I only manage to scramble away a few feet. He's faster than he should be, considering his condition, and my hair is a liability.

He gets his gnarled fingers tangled in it easily, and he jerks me to a halt. It wrenches my neck and I yelp, lifting my hands instinctively to try to relieve the pressure. He drags me back toward him, a nasty smile on his face. "Go ahead. Say 'thank you, Puck,' for ending your poor, cowardly little life."

I shake my head — or try to — tears spilling down my cheeks as I feel several strands of hair separate from my scalp. I'm not thanking him for this. I'm *not*, no matter what he does to me. I need to stay strong — for myself, but also for Daddy.

"You know," the wix muses, lifting his other hand to my face. His fingers are scratchy and rough, and they reek like rotten eggs. "Daddy *has* always had good taste."

Something about the way he says it makes the panic in my chest grow even stronger. I try again to pull away, but he clamps his fingers into my cheeks, keeping me in place. His nails are long and sharp.

"Stop squirming, dog," Puck snaps, and no matter how frail he looks, he's clearly stronger than I am. He uses his weight to push me down farther.

I'm forced to let go of the grip I had in my hair — the only thing stopping *his* grip from becoming unbearable — to catch myself, crying out as my palms land on something hard and sharp, like gravel.

Thankfully, he lets go of my hair. Before I can do more than breathe a sigh of relief, he slides his dirty, wrinkled fingers over my lips. I clamp them shut, biting my teeth together so hard my jaw aches.

"Open up, puppy dog. Show me your pretty pearly whites," the wix says in a creepy, sing-song voice. I try to shake my head, unwilling to open my mouth. I only budge it a fraction of inches, but it's enough to get my point across.

If he wants my mouth open, he's going to have to *make* me. I'm not doing it for him.

Puck just laughs. "So you *do* have a spine. I was beginning to wonder. I knew Daddy couldn't have changed *that* much in only ten years." The wix pauses, lowering his brows for a moment. "Eleven?" After a second, he shrugs, his rheumy eyes meeting mine again. "Either way, we're going to have fun together, mutt. I've always wanted to play with Daddy's toys... It's just a pity for *you* that I've never quite learned to play nice."

Then he smiles, and every one of his yellow teeth is a caution sign.

He shoves me again, forcing me to my back, then he plants his foot on my chest. The tread of his boot bites into my skin, reminding me of my nudity. I try to cover my penis, but he shifts his foot to kick my hand away, threatening to crush it under the heavy sole until I yank it back.

"No point in hiding, dog. Not much there to hide anyway, is there?" He stares pointedly at my crotch, and despite the chill in the warehouse sending goosebumps across my skin, I feel myself heat with embarrassment.

I've been naked before, many times. It's a part of life for us werewolves and not something I've ever been ashamed of. But the only person who has ever looked at me like *that* was Daddy, and it had never felt like *this*. The derision, the judgment...making me feel small and worthless.

Making me feel dirty.

A lump forms in my throat, threatening to choke me, and I force myself to swallow it, though tears burn my eyes. I need to stay strong for Daddy. Levi's going to find me, and when he does, I can't be *broken*. He won't want me then.

He won't want you now. The thought hits me too quick to ward against, and my flinch is hard.

The wix laughs, grinding his foot on my chest again. I try to dislodge him but I'm *weak*—too weak to fight free from an old man. Maybe Beta was right all those times he'd told me I was worthless, useless, a drain on the pack resources.

Maybe I should have just let him kill me then.

Immediately, my wolf revolts inside me. I might feel like giving up, but he's not ready to die yet. He snaps his teeth at my ribcage, and I can almost hear him snarling at me to pull myself together.

"You're pathetic," I say, desperate to distract the wix. Maybe if I get him angry enough, he'll beat me instead. "No wonder Daddy didn't want you anymore."

His fingers freeze on the clasp of his dirty brown robe. "What did you say?" Puck's voice sends ice down my spine, but I lick my lips and repeat myself.

"I...I said you're pathetic, and Daddy was right to...to kick you out. You're just jealous he doesn't want you anymore." My own voice is shaky, and I think he must realize I'm stalling for time, because the anger on his face morphs to a smirk instead.

"Aw, so the *widdle puppy* has teeth, does he? Leaving Daddy—and *I* left *him*, I'll have you know—was the best thing I ever did for myself. If I'd stayed, I'd be nothing more than his cumdump. Just a hole, like *you*. Now, let's see if *your* hole is as good for me as it is for Daddy."

* * * *

Daddy

The goons from the BAA are less than careful as they transport me down the elevator and into the black van waiting outside. Granted, my body is essentially living stone at this point, so the few knocks to the head I get don't hurt, but they *do* stoke the flames of my anger.

Every second they take to remove the tourmaline stake is a second *longer* it's going to take for me to metabolize the toxin and regain the ability to move—which means it's another second longer my boy is stuck with that…that…

I can't even think of a strong enough insult.

The Puck I saw today was not the one from my memories. If he hadn't dared lay a finger on Eryn, I might have felt pity for what he's turned into. When he'd fled a decade ago, he'd been a youthful twenty-nine, though even then I'd started to see the signs that he was reaching the limits of his magic.

I'd tried warning him, but he'd refused to listen, always pushing himself too much, too fast…using magic for things he could have done without. Always pestering me to borrow my *Focus*, then pouting when I refused.

Puck wouldn't listen when I tried to explain that the tool was only that…a *tool*. It could help direct magical energy more efficiently, but it didn't *create* magic. It still had to pull from *somewhere*.

For me, it isn't a problem. My own magic is boundless—gathered from the air around me and the blood I drink, replenishing itself faster than I could ever hope to use it. The *Focus* just lets me direct that energy into spells. Without it, I'm basically an overcharged battery, too powerful for anyone to tap.

For him, though… I suspect I know what happened. I'd bet my liver that he'd tried channeling too much energy through the *Focus*. Now look what it did to him—an old man at nearly forty.

I hate to think what he could be doing to my precious Eryn right at this second. He'd always been a jealous boy—and a selfish one, too. Constantly throwing tantrums, teasing the servants...anything he could think of to get my attention, except asking for it.

The final straw in our relationship had been when I'd caught him experimenting on one of my feeders in the hopes of stealing her magic. I'll never forget the poor selkie's face. She'd died shortly afterward.

He'd insisted it had been for 'research' and that the breakthrough would revolutionize magic use forever. I'd called it torture. If only I hadn't let my feelings for him blind me. I'd thought it love, then, but now, after my time with Eryn, I'm not so sure. I'd believed him when he said he would go peacefully with the BAA for sentencing if I just kissed him one last time. Everything in me had said it was a bad idea, but I'd ignored my instincts.

Then, he'd staked me with tourmaline before stealing my *Focus* and fleeing, leaving me to rot. If Maggie hadn't found me the next morning, who knows how long it would have taken me to recover.

If he'd been willing to skin that poor selkie just to see what her magic would do, what is he doing to Eryn right now?

Chapter Two

Pet

The old wix shifts his weight forward, putting even more pressure on my chest, and starts to unlace his dirty brown robes. I try to buck him off, thrashing and howling, but it just makes him laugh.

"It's so cute to watch you try. *Pointless,* but cute." Puck flashes his yellow teeth at me as his robe gapes open.

His chest is pockmarked, scattered with liver spots, and his stomach is saggy and wrinkled where it's tucked into yellow sweatpants. Vomit burns my throat at the sight. It's not that he's unattractive — though he is — it's that I *don't want this.* He could be a supermodel and I'd feel the same disgust.

He starts to shove down his pants, and I turn my head, refusing to look. I lock my gaze on the red warding scribbled across the warehouse door instead. A hexagram at the center of a Solar Cross, an *omega* sign at the base and a triangle at the top, like a hat. It threatens to draw out a hysterical laugh, but only for a moment.

Only until the wix takes his foot off my chest... I gasp in a breath, swamped with an unwanted feeling of relief as the weight lifts off. The rush of oxygen makes me dizzy.

I close my eyes for a second, trying to still the spinning room, but then his weight returns, less sharp this time, like it's been more evenly distributed. Instinctively, I look to see him kneeling astride me, his hand raised. The sound of the *slap* echoes through the warehouse before the pain flares through my cheek. I cry out, clutching my face. He smacks me again, knocking my hand back to the cement in a jarring strike. Then, he takes advantage of my briefly opened mouth. Two fingers dig their way inside until I gag.

They taste of garlic and ammonia. Tears burn my eyes, and I don't mean to—or at least, I don't *think* I mean to—but I bite down until I taste copper. The old wix screams, yanking his fingers free.

"Fuck!" he curses, lifting his hand again.

Before he can, what sounds like an air raid siren goes off in the warehouse. I have a moment of euphoria— *they've found me*, I think, until I see the pulsing red lines starting to burn on the floor, growing brighter and longer until they've formed a pentagram.

The wix lowers his hand to my cheek. "Lucky bitch," he says, squeezing tight enough to hurt my jaw before he stands. I whimper, curling up on my side and cradling my face with my palm.

For the space of a single heartbeat, hope glimmers. He's walking away. I could stand and run. Maybe the warding wouldn't stop me, since they are already screaming out a warning. Or, maybe they'd at least kill me and put me out of my misery, removing the ability of the old wix to use me as a bargaining chip in his petty revenge on Daddy.

Before I can do more than sit up and roll to my hands and knees, though, the bastard is back, a heavy iron collar clutched in his arthritic hands. I start to struggle, trying to pull myself backward along the cement, but he's too fast, and his fingers are surprisingly nimble.

He has the collar clasped around my neck before I can scramble far enough away. It clicks ominously, louder even than the screaming siren from the wards, and he tightens it to the point of pain. After wearing a collar for Daddy, it shouldn't feel so foreign, but everything about it is…*wrong*. The metal is too cold, too tight.

"Oh, and I know what you're thinking." Puck straightens back up. "But don't worry. When I broke that ugly gold collar, I used a hex to nullify that pesky little contract you had. If you're expecting it to kick in and send you back to that silly Flesh Market, you'll be disappointed."

I wasn't thinking about that at all, but now that he's pointed it out, I realize I should have been. Knowing it's not an option makes me wish he hadn't said anything at all.

I feel like I can barely breathe, and I claw at the collar, but all I succeed in doing is scratching the skin of my throat. I give up on it and look to the thick, heavy chain stretching from a D-ring perched above my Adam's apple to a bolt on the cinderblock wall. I yank on it instead, tugging with all my feeble might.

It does nothing but make the wix laugh. The old bastard pats my head as he strolls away, saying, "Good puppy. Wear yourself out for me, why don't you?"

"Fuck!" I curse and collapse back to the cement, lightheaded.

"Massssster," a snakelike voice hisses behind me, and it takes me a second to recognize it. I cringe and twist around, my gaze locking with the icy stare of the child-like monster that had attacked Levi back in the hotel.

The demon—if that's what it is, since it looks nothing like the crimson-skinned, glowing-eyed monsters from the storybooks—is standing in the now-finished pentacle just inside the door. Its paper-pale skin looks a *bit* red, but I realize quickly it's from the flashing lights of the wards.

The genderless creature bares its hundred teeth at me, and I shudder back, though I only move a few paces before the chain tightens too far and stops me. I swear the creature laughs.

"I told you not to port in here. Didn't I tell you not to do that?" the wix snaps as he stomps over to the pentagram and, with an angry slash of his shoe, breaks the fiery line. Immediately, the warding goes quiet, and the silence is almost painfully loud after the screeching.

"I have failed, Massssster," the creature hisses. I'm not familiar with it enough to be certain, but if I had to guess, I'd say it looks…proud of itself. There is a certain tilt to its lips, a glimmer in its black eyes.

Puck must notice the same expressions that I do, because rage darkens his face. "How? I gave you specific instructions. I gave you a fucking *blueprint,* for Christ's sake!"

The creature cringes. "That *word,* Massssster!"

"Oh, you don't like it? Does it hurt your widdle brain?" The wix laughs. "I've always wondered how the *Christians,* of all people, managed to stumble on just the right combination of letters to weaken a species as allegedly powerful as *yours*. Did one of your kind fuck up—or was it just a coincidence?"

Now, the creature looks angry, and the more emotion that crosses its face, the more it real it—they—seem. No longer just a murderous paper doll... I have a growing suspicion that even though they wear no chains, they're just as trapped as I am, a puppet in a crazy man's show.

"Fine. If you want something done right, do it yourself. That's what my mama always said." The wix buttons up his robe, and the tight fear in my chest uncoils slightly. "Be a good little slave and watch the place, hm-mm?"

The creature gives a minuscule bow, but as they bend, I see the corner of their lips twitch. "Yessss, Massssster. As you command, sssso I musssst do."

The wix laughs and pats them on the head like a child. The creature's little smile dies. The wix just taps the wall by the door before he opens it, the red warding fading while he leaves. As soon as he tugs it closed behind him, the warding snaps back, glowing brighter than ever.

And now, I'm alone with the monster...whose attention is now fully focused.

On me.

* * * *

Princeling

"This is a bad idea," I say to Amanda Graves, my supervisor, as I stand at attention across from her in her office.

Director Graves purses her lips. "If you have a better one, Aries, then share it. Until then, go do your job."

"If we continue to detain him, we're condemning his bonded to a likely torturous death at the hands of a man who has already proven he cares little for human life. It goes against everything this agency stands for. Eryn is just a civilian," I argue, struggling to keep my argument rational.

I'm biased — she *knows* I'm biased — but I can't stand the thought of leaving the helpless little wolf in the hands of a deranged lunatic any longer than we have to. I'd be cringing even if he *weren't* my best friend's lover...but he *is*.

Director Graves shoves a loose piece of paper into the folder she's compiling, the motion harsh before she meets my gaze again. "And if we *don't* continue to detain Leviathan, we'll be setting him loose on an entire city of innocent civilians. You know as well as I do what damage a Bloodwraith on a rampage would cause. And that's not even factoring in his bloody *aura*. The last thing we need is another '72."

I cringe at the reminder. No one could forget the riots of 2072. Just after the Collapse, with new Elyries being forced into the spotlight every day, it had been a violent time. After a young Bloodwraith, only in his fifth or sixth century of life, had been threatened with deportation for feeding on Blanks in public, he'd retaliated by unraveling his aura. At his age, it hadn't been particularly strong, just enough to affect a single city block in Chicago.

By the end of the day, however, every hospital in the city had been out of beds, and the morgue was overflowing with corpses.

"He's not a youngling anymore, Amanda. He can control himself," I say in defense of my friend, though even I wonder if it's true in this case. I've never seen Levi like this, not with any of his feeders, nor with his boys. Eryn is…different. Special.

"You don't know that. I can't take the risk." Amanda closes the folder on her desk and raps the bottom on the table to straighten the papers, a clear sign that our conversation is over. "Return to your beat. Maybe, if we find this bastard soon enough, we can mitigate some of the fallout."

I give a quick salute, knowing better than to continue pressing now, and step out of the room. Her mind is made up, and I can't honestly say I blame her. If we let him out and it goes wrong, the blood will be just as much on our hands as it will be on his.

The public's trust in the Bureau of Arcane Activity is already only hanging on by a thread. Every year, we have to fight to convince the individual states of the American Coalition that it is in their best interest to continue funding us for another few months. And every year, a few states threaten to close their purses.

As I take the elevator to the lower floor that the Barracks are on, I curse the stupidity of Blanks. Their memories are short and fragile if they've already forgotten the chaos the world had fallen into before we formed.

The BAA is the only justice system for us Elyries. We handle everything from routine paperwork and registration to crime management and relocation. The Blanks have no system to deal with our kind. Their prisons would kill half our species and be useless for those remaining. Their courts can't understand the nuances of our cultures—how an *ankhuban* can survive on consensual feedings, but an *incubus* can't.

It's one reason we have Flesh Markets, a concept that still horrifies the Blanks.

Without the BAA, the entire system would fall apart. Peace between our species is as fragile as a house of cards—and as real as a house of mirrors.

Peace. I scoff at the thought as I storm—not literally, though, since as a *leonan sidhe,* my power is not that of the elements—into the barracks to gather my gear. I roll my eyes at the holo in the corner, playing yet another advertisement praising the Coalition's work in blending our communities—how gun violence has gone down, and crime is at an all-time low.

Of course it is. Their police only report Blank-on-Blank crime, which has nearly disappeared. Not completely, of course, there would always be muggers and thieves, but their petty squabbles over skin color and gender must have seemed pointless in the face of so many new peoples to hate.

So, sure, the news anchor might be right. Crime has decreased. Humankind is nearly 'at peace' with each other. There hasn't been a war between nations in nearly fifty years. But every day, I have to go scrape a selkie out of an oil slick or help a wereshifter dig out a silver bullet. The local Kiss of vampires had a glass manufacturer on retainer to replace their shattered windows, and our kind is legally required to keep special insurance if we want to own a business, just to fix repairs from damage done by Humans-First protestors—as if our kind isn't struggling enough already to scrape together coins.

Yeah, this 'peace' feels a lot like a silent war.

I strap on my sidearms. The first, a new iron-free Smith and Wesson made almost entirely out of a new blend of carbon-fiber and titanium is my primary weapon, loaded with nonlethal ammo capable of taking down most Elyries—each UV-treated clay bullet filled with a blend of just enough liquid silver, iron dust and salt to incapacitate.

My backup weapon is a Glock that I've never had to use. It holds seven rounds, each different, and each lethal to one of several species. If my first or second shot doesn't take a combatant down, the third will. Solid silver for weres, wood for the vamps and salted iron for the rest—which is why my holster is a thick, treated leather. It's an extra barrier to protect myself from exposure to the toxins.

I adjust the guns on my hips and close my eyes, sending a wish into the universe that my luck holds. *Let the Glock stay holstered. Let us keep the peace.*

I feel a whisper of a breeze kiss the base of my neck, though the barracks have no windows and I'd closed the door behind me. I press two fingers to my lips in gratitude, then close my locker.

Back to the streets.

Chapter Three

Pet

"What are you?" I ask the creature, hoping if I get them talking maybe they won't eat me.

"It sssseeeems your Daddy hassss neglected your...education," the creature says with a grin, moving closer. Their movement is creepy, a stuttering, sliding gait that, despite the legs, reminds me of a snake.

"What do you mean?" I don't understand, and only part of me truly cares for the answer. I strain to scoot farther away but the chain is stretched taut. The creature lifts a six-fingered hand and runs it over the links, their nails scraping over the rusted metal.

"It wassss bad enough when the Leviathan abandoned ussss for thissss usssselessss world." The creature stops just out of reach, anger crawling over their face again. The way he says it, 'the' Leviathan, like...like it's a title? And the way everyone kept calling Daddy 'Prince'... My heart skips in my chest.

Something tells me that my Daddy isn't a common vampire. To be fair, never once did he claim he *was*. I assumed, because he drinks blood and lives in a gothic castle and...oh, *shit*. He really *isn't* a vampire, which means... I swallow, pushing down the growing sense of dread.

Vampire or demon, it doesn't matter. He's still my Daddy, and knowing his species isn't quite what I thought shouldn't change that. *Right?*

"But now, to know he hassssn't even sssspoken of ussss to his whore." The creature shakes his head. "Dissssgraceful."

"I... Are you a demon?" I ask, my voice quiet and shaky. What I'm really asking is if *Daddy* is a demon, a creature that has haunted my nightmares since I was a pup.

Will it change anything if the creature confirms it?

For a second, fear clamps around my chest like a vise. A demon, in my bed every night, with his fangs in my throat...but then the fear dissipates. Leviathan *might* be a demon...but he's taken better care of me than anyone else ever has.

"Yessss," the creature hisses. "You may call me Whissssper." I know enough about demons to know better than to assume that's their name. Like the fae, they are fiercely protective of it, at least according to the storybooks.

"I'm...I'm Eryn," I offer, hoping it will buy me some goodwill. And if not that, at least a little time.

"I don't care." Suddenly, Whisper grins and tightens their hand around the chain until it shatters.

I stare dumbly at the now-broken links for a second before I scramble to my feet. "Why?" I ask, looking between the door — my *freedom* — and the Whisper. As long as the wards are only for alerting, not stopping, I can get out.

"My *Masssster*," Whisper growls the words with such anger that my suspicion that they weren't here by their own choice is confirmed, "has ordered me to *'watch the place'*." Their sudden grin is nearly manic but still threatening, considering the sheer number of razor-sharp teeth on display. "Sssso I think I shall watch it burn. Run away, little wolf, and run quick. My Masssster won't be pleasssssed to find you missssing."

I open my mouth, gratitude overflowing, but the demon hisses, lifting a finger to stop the words about to spill out. "Don't thank me, or my Masssster will use the debt to call you back like an unruly dog, your tail between your legs."

I snap my mouth closed and give a sharp nod to show I understand. Then I hurry to the door.

"On second thought," Whisper says, their voice chilling, then strong hands grab me from behind. One of them curls around my mouth, pressing something solid and hard against it. "Open up, little wolf," the demon singsongs, pressing harder until I have no choice but to obey or risk shattering my teeth with the object.

It tastes of nothing, and I barely get a feel of the shape — smooth and unfaceted — before Whisper grips my hair and yanks my head back. The object — a stone, I'm guessing, from the shape, and I don't know why my mind gets stuck on that now — gets lodged in my throat and I start to choke.

"Swallow, dog. Be a good bitch," Whisper murmurs, and a moist, slug-like thing — their tongue — drags over my ear. I shudder and something about the movement must open my throat just enough. The stone slides down, and I'm able to swallow.

I cough, the feeling painful and sharp. "Why?" I whine, my voice rough and ragged.

"My Masssster will be angry to find one of his toyssss missing. You better run fassssst, little wolf." Whisper laughs. "Four legssss would be fassssster than two."

"I can't shift!" I admit with a yelp, my panic spreading. I wish the wolfsbane were still in my system, or Daddy were here to talk me through it. I wish for many things that can't happen.

"I've alwayssss found fear to be a great motivator to learn," Whisper says, then they yank me around, slamming my back into the cinderblocks. They are shorter than me and smaller, but I have no doubt who will win in a fight.

"Shift, little wolf." Whisper stretches closer, their hundred-tooth mouth close enough to my skin I can feel their icy breath. "Shift, or I will rape you and eat you."

Whisper, apparently, is right.

Fear is a great motivator.

My wolf rears, consuming me from the inside out. I fall forward, four paws striking the cement. The iron collar must be magic, because it is still there, tight around mine and the wolf's throat.

The wolf starts growling, its teeth bared at the larger predator, who only laughs and rips the door from the hinges.

Out, my wolf howls, and I agree with him. *Yes, out...*I urge him.

"Run fassssst, little wolf," Whisper calls after me, their voice already fading in the distance as my wolf and I flee into the city, following the scent of greenery and growing things.

With waxing Goddess Moon above us, we run. Free now, I feel my eyes closing inside the wolf's body as he grows stronger, but I swear I hear the beast speak to me.

Sleep, he says, the sound like birdsong in the wind. *Safe now.*

* * * *

Princeling

My comm is mostly static in my ear. I press my thumb to the bud and work it in a bit deeper, then say, "Did not copy. Please repeat. Did not copy." Service out here in the parks is spotty at best, especially off the main trails. I can't exactly waltz back to the streets, though, not after getting another tip of a wolf sighting. Our teams have only been searching the park for half an hour, barely enough time to skirt the border.

It would be easier if we knew what Eryn's were-form looked like, of course. So far, we've passed off six dogs, three coyotes and a very large cat over to animal control.

The officer's voice is a bit clearer this time. "There's—break-in—Guggenheim—alarms."

I hear enough to catch the gist. Another break-in at a museum, this time the Guggenheim. We'd put an alert out to the museums weeks ago, warning them of a potential theft, and a few of them have voluntarily closed their doors to the public while we try to catch the perpetrator, but most have refused.

I can't blame them. With no clue who, until now, is behind the robberies, and still no idea what Puck is after, we can't give them a timeline to reopen, and they lose money for every day they stay shuttered.

"I'm sending a team now," I say in my comm, then pull out my cellular to send out the order. I hesitate after I send it, then send out a second, reallocating two of the three teams to the robbery. The last one, I split into three, two-man teams to cover the south, west and east quadrants of the park.

Instead of continuing to search for tracks to follow, I turn my ATV North. If I'm lucky, my supervisor will give me enough time to continue the search, but I doubt it. I suspect that by mid-morning, she'll pull me back to the robberies, and we'll be forced to leave Eryn to his fate.

With limited time, I can't afford to waste any. While I hope that the wolf that was spotted, described by the panicked caller as a *"white beast with glowing red eyes"* is Levi's pet, I have my doubts. If my suspicions are correct, I suspect the caller spotted a member of the local werewolf pack.

The city had reluctantly ceded the rights to the poorly named Hunter Island Sanctuary almost a century ago. Too many shifters were getting arrested for roaming the city on the full moon, unwilling to stay cooped up in their dens any longer. The initial proposal by the government had been to build a new, larger detention facility to hold the 'rogue wereshifters' in.

The Alpha of the local pack, however, had threatened to bring a discrimination suit against the city. Everyone knew he'd lose the case, but it would have still cost the city more to fight it—and build the detention center—than to give in. So, they'd compromised. The Brooklyn Pack got a portion of the parklands, a heavily forested patch of almost-wild to run in, and they agreed to keep out of the city.

For the most part, the shifters had stuck to their end of the bargain, but it wouldn't be the first time we'd had a young werewolf too curious for his own good. We pick up at least a few a year. I've delivered a handful of the unruly pups back to the Alpha myself.

It's one of the reasons I'm heading to the pack alone. Ever since they got a new Alpha about a decade ago, things have changed. The pack has grown wary of outsiders and leery of the BAA most of all. Our bi-annual visits to their territory to verify that they are following all the regulations — particularly the law regarding breeding rights — have become tense and uncomfortable.

I've always hated the law restricting packs to two breeding pairs per year, but it's not my place to pick and choose what laws I enforce.

I hope that I'm wrong, and I find the boy, but if I'm not, it's better that I approach the pack alone.

I'm approaching the outer boundary of the pack's territory when my comm goes off in my ear. " —er Aries? Report—base—ly. I repeat. Com—Ies. Re—back to—immed…"

I sigh and turn my ATV around, my heart sinking in my chest. For his sake, I hope the wolf *was* Eryn. At least that means he's free of Puck.

Chapter Four

Pet
The next evening…Saturday

I wake, naked and screaming, to my ribs shattering. The sound is barely out of my mouth when they heal, and I fall to my hands and knees. *Hands*, I realize, and start to feel for my wolf. He's curled up in my chest, whining. Whining? I've never felt anything from him but anger or exhausted contentment. If I have to guess, I would almost think he feels…guilty?

My vision is blurry, so I rub my eyes, trying to blink away the fog as I look around. Slowly, the film clears.

Terror cinches around my belly. "No, no, no…." I mutter, scrambling up onto my knees. All around me are cinderblock walls, except for the metal door. It has a small glass window near the top, too high to peer out of unless I were to stand on my tiptoes and strain. Even then, I doubt I'd be able to see much.

It doesn't stop me from trying. But when I do, all I can see is the top of the wall across from me, *more gray cinderblocks.*

Did the old wix catch me? Is that why my wolf feels guilty? These walls look different—less chipped and dirty, but he could have moved me. I'd only seen one room. Maybe my escape meant he had to go somewhere else? Somewhere even harder to flee from?

What if no one could find me?

Fear clamps down on my chest like a stone, and I grapple for the door handle, yanking and twisting with no luck. It's locked, and no amount of pulling budges it.

My head tells me to bang on the door and holler, hope someone—*anyone*—will come. I don't want to be alone in this room, this cell that reminds me of too many nightmares, too many bad memories.

My instincts, though, tell me to huddle in the corner, stay quiet, stay still. Don't draw attention. Maybe he'll forget about me. Starving to death would surely be less painful than whatever the old wix has planned.

Neither option is a smart one. Instead, I pace along the walls, looking for weaknesses—cracks in the mortar, a hidden window...and if not, maybe a weapon. A nail or a forgotten spoon, anything I can use to defend myself.

Nothing.

I don't even want to sit down. The cement floor is dirty, covered in dust and loose gravel, and even as I'm considering it, I see a centipede skitter along the base of the wall. I'm naked as the day I was born. The thought of it on my bare skin...? I shudder and crouch in the center of the floor instead, balancing on the balls of my feet and wrapping my arms around my shoulders. I tuck my face and try to concentrate.

The iron collar seems to tighten around my throat as my breath comes faster.

Letting the panic grow will only make this worse. I need to stay calm and hope I get another chance to escape. Maybe Whisper will come back and let me go a second time. If so, I'll have to be faster, or smarter, or both.

I don't know how long I'm crouching there. It feels like days—my feet are aching from the position, and my skin is freezing—but I know it can't have been. Suddenly, a sound startles me, and I scramble back toward the wall, no longer caring about the gravel or bugs in the face of a more immediate threat.

The man—*werewolf,* my inner beast snarls—who enters is unfamiliar. His scent is strange on my nose, stirring up memories of my old pack, even though he isn't one of them. Instinctively, I settle farther into my crouch, fisting my hands in front of my chest. Little good they would do, though, as large as he is. As *small* as I am.

"Well, well. You're a right little beastie," the man drawls, his accent strange to my ears. On another day, in another place, I might have found it pretty. "You got a name?"

He sounds kind, curious…but my inner wolf is snarling at me not to trust him. For the first time in my life, I listen to him and bare my flat, human teeth. He just laughs.

"Feisty, aren't ya? Prettier than I expected, too." The stranger steps fully inside and closes the door behind him, locking himself inside the cell with me. I scramble along the wall to the corner as he approaches. I hate being backed into it, but at least I'll have something solid at my back and sides. *Maybe it will help.*

He just laughs and stops at the center of the room, still too close to me for comfort. He looks deceptively unthreatening with his ginger hair and scattering of freckles across his nose and cheeks. "Now, now, little pup. No need to be like that, I ain't gonna hurt ya."

I dig my teeth into my cheek, weighing my options until I realize that I don't have many. "Who are you?" I ask, hating that my voice comes out so soft and high. I sound like a child, not like a threat.

"My name is Brenton Dixon, I'm Alpha of this pack," he answers with a *laissez-faire* grin. Maybe he thinks it will make me trust him. It doesn't. If he *really* wanted me to trust him, he'd tell me the name of the pack. Better yet, I'd have woken in a room with a bed and an unlocked door.

Hearing he's the Alpha of whatever pack I ended up in only has me tensing more. I tip my head down, shielding my neck. From the way his eyes narrow, I know he notices, but he doesn't say anything about it.

Instead, he just takes another step closer, his shadow falling across my legs. I sink lower. "Tell me your name," he says, "and I'll get you a plate of food, something to drink." Again, that cajoling tone, that winsome smile.

I shake my head. "Just let me out, I didn't do nothing! You can't keep me here!"

Dixon laughs then he's suddenly moving, tangling his fist in my hair to drag me up onto my knees. I grapple for his wrist but am not strong enough to yank free. "How would *you* know what you did? Feral, that's what you are." He leans down, his face inches from mine, so close I can smell his breath. It smells of cherries.

One hand still in my hair, he slides the thick fingers of his other one along my collar. "Did you break your chains, little pup? Was your pack protecting you from the Council's judgment?"

I shake my head. "I'm not... No one was *protecting* me." No one but Daddy, but he's gone now. My heart pains at the thought of him still lying there, on the floor of a hotel room, that black stake still...still... A sob pours from my mouth. "I just want to go home. I didn't do anything wrong."

"You don't remember nothing of last night, do ya?"

Tears burn my eyes as I'm forced to shake my head and admit it. "Please, just let me go," I beg, wishing I was strong enough to fight free—or smart enough to talk my way out of it.

Instead, I'm just as weak as ever. What does Levi even see in me? Maybe he *won't* try to find me. Maybe he'll just...move on to the next boy who catches his eye.

Inside, my wolf wakes, growling and snapping. His mind is faint and sluggish, but I can just catch the edge of his thoughts, the denial. It seems my wolf has claimed Daddy as his, too, and *he's* not willing to give up on him, not yet.

"Now why would I do that?" Dixon sounds amused as he answers, loosening his grip on my hair just enough that it's no longer painful. The pain returns as soon as I start struggling harder.

Slowly, a realization has been forming in my mind and now it fully clicks. If he's a pack Alpha, then I haven't been recaptured by the old wix...*which means he's still out there*. Panic floods me and I gasp, redoubling my efforts to get free.

There's a phantom heat in my belly when I think of the ruby stone sitting there, waiting...biding its time for the old wix to find me. Will he kill me first? Or just sink his sharp nailed hand in my belly to tear it free?

My scalp screams in pain as I yank against the Alpha's grip, and I don't know if it's the pained whimpers spilling from my mouth or just that he doesn't want to damage me yet, but Dixon releases my hair, curling his hands around my throat and pinning me to the cement on my back instead.

"Calm down," he growls, and I can feel the weight of his aura on my skin. It's cloying and hot, but just like with my last pack, it does nothing to calm my wolf. It only seems to piss him off.

Pain, throbbing like a toothache, fills my fingertips as my wolf's claws split through the skin. I scrabble at him to get free, the sharp nails leaving behind red, bleeding welts on Dixon's forearms.

He curses but doesn't let go. Instead, he tightens his fist on my throat until I can't breathe and grabs my wrists with his other hand, pinning them down. He drops his knee on my lower stomach, using his weight and the resulting pain to keep me still. "Like I said," he growls, "*feral.*"

I feel lightheaded as I struggle to breathe, but he doesn't let go. My vision goes spotted black around the edges and my mouth opens like a fish, gasping at air with no luck. I try to buck, to yank myself free, but my body goes limp and boneless, and I sag to the floor.

The dark claims me.

* * * *

Daddy
Sunday

Finally, the morning after the BAA bastards removed the tourmaline from my heart, I can feel the

34

toxin receding. It starts with a tingling in my fingers and toes, until the light tingles turn into a strong buzzing, like thousands of bees are trapped under my skin.

I grit my teeth as the feeling spreads and examine the cell I've been stuck inside instead. Not that I don't already know what it looks like — tourmaline-backed mirrored walls, floors made of the same solid black material, lit by holy fire sconces.

After all, I helped design these cells, back when they were first being built. Centuries of research has turned me into the leading expert on Elyries in the world. There's no one alive who knows more about the individual species than I do. It's why they hired me.

My lips twitch in a smile, though I find no humor in the situation. They shouldn't have trusted me nearly as much as they had. Like I would have been stupid enough to design a cell and *not* leave myself a way out?

Granted, my 'way out' isn't going to be easy or simple. I *also* hadn't been stupid enough to make the escape route obvious enough that any other random demon locked up here could stumble on it.

It's going to take power — and a lot of it.

And drawing in that much energy would have consequences I won't be able to avoid. Namely, an unraveling of my aura strong enough to coat the entire city and a subsequent hunger I'd be forced to quench — not to mention, being completely out of my mind in bloodlust for an indeterminate amount of time.

It's not going to be ideal, but I'm not stupid enough to think that Aries will convince the BAA to let me go. I'm not even convinced that he's going to try. He knows me too well to think that I will just sit back and let Puck follow through with whatever he's planning, not while he has my Eryn.

I'm still mostly immobile when the door to my cell buzzes, the lock tumbling. It opens and Aries — my best friend and current backstabber, though not literally — steps inside. The tall Black man looks upset as he stares down at me.

"You have every right to hate me," he says in lieu of a greeting.

"No *'how are you doing, Levi?'*" I say with a groan, my voice dry and raspy. "Not even a *'Lovely day out there'*?"

"You know this isn't what I want," Aries says, ignoring my weak attempt at humor. He sets a small stack of folded white clothing on the floor by the door.

"And yet...here we are." Gritting my teeth, I try to sit up. My muscles scream and only some of them work, so by the time I'm half slumped in a seated position, my brow is sweaty, and I feel sick.

"I promise we're doing everything we can to find him, Levi." Aries crouches down in front of me, and the sympathy on his face feels so *fucking* condescending.

I turn away. "Unless you're here to tell me you found him or bring me someone to drink from, leave. Your face is annoying me."

He sighs, but eventually, he seems to realize that I don't have anything else to say to him. He stands and heads for the door.

Just before he leaves, he gives me one last, hangdog look, an expression that doesn't sit well on his unusually solemn face. "We *will* find him."

I drop back to the ground to conserve my energy. I'll get dressed later, when more of the tourmaline has worn off. Until then, though, I close my eyes and allow my—not soul, us demons don't have those. Essence, maybe?—to creep out.

Weak and still poisoned, it doesn't get far. But it does get just far enough to tangle into the core of the prisoner next to me like a parasite, draining off kernels of energy one tiny bit at a time. The effort is enough to make me sag, but I'm smiling.

One down.

A hundred more to go.

Daddy's coming, Pet.

Chapter Five

Pet
Sunday midday

I wake up in a bed, groggy and sore, to the sound of grunting interspersed with a wet, slapping sound it takes me seconds to recognize. I sit up with a gasp, looking around me in horror.

I'm alone, but I'm not in the empty cement cell anymore. The walls are cinderblock, and there are no windows, and there is still a metal door on the far wall, but it doesn't even have a handle on the inside.

This room, though plain, has actual furniture. I'm sitting in the middle of a large bed — bigger than the one in my room at the packhouse, and *definitely* bigger than the bed in the Blue Room, but not as big as Daddy's bed at home. There's no dresser, but there is a plush purple rug in the center of the floor that matches the threadbare comforter.

It takes me a second to get my bearings, but I realize that the sounds of someone fucking are coming through the wall on the left of the bed. At first, I only hear the grunting, but then faintly beneath it I notice the whimpers—little pained cries that have fear clenching at my chest. I don't know where I am, or why...but I suspect it's for nothing good.

I roll off the bed and land painfully on my knees before I scramble to my feet, sprinting to the door. I start to bang on it, the sound echoing. "Let me out! Hey! Someone let me out!"

I hear footsteps and my hopes rise—until they shatter. All the person does is bang on the door and holler, "Shut up in there!"

"Please, just let me out!" I keep hitting the door. I don't know what else to do. Staying quiet might be a smarter choice, but it's not like the lack of sound will make them forget about me. I almost wish they'd just...do whatever they are planning on and get it over with.

"Knock it off!" The man bangs on the door again but still doesn't open it.

A soft sound from the wall on the right finally makes me freeze. It comes again, barely loud enough to hear. Heart thudding, I cross the rug and huddle against it, trying to hear.

The voice is young and male. "You gotta stop," he's saying, over and over. Even without seeing him, I can hear his fear.

"What is this place?" I say back, trying to stay quiet but still loud enough he can hear me through the wall. I don't even know how the sound is coming through in the first place, until I notice the crumbling mortar between some of the cinderblocks.

He goes quiet, for long enough I fear he won't answer. Finally, though, he says, "The Brooklyn Pack Mollyhouse."

"I don't...what's a mollyhouse?" I've never heard of the Brooklyn Pack, but that doesn't mean anything. Most of the Northeast packs are small and steadily shrinking, thanks to the whelping restrictions, and Alpha had made sure our pack had been self-sufficient. I'd never been invited to the few inter-pack gatherings he'd authorized.

I used to be happy to be excluded, but now, as the boy answers, I find myself regretting it. If I'd been allowed to go, maybe this wouldn't be such a surprise.

"Where all the omegas and mollys live," the boy answers immediately, his voice matter-of-fact, like it's something I should already know. Maybe I should, but I'm certain that my old pack didn't have one of these, whatever it is—just the packhouse and several cabins for mated pairs. Then again, we also had only had two omegas, and both were barely more than pups, so maybe that was why?

"What's a molly?" Since I'm not an omega, they must think I'm whatever that is.

"A beta, for the alphas who want to fuck but aren't interested in breeding," he explains. His voice gets softer, bleeding pain, as he adds, "We lost our last one a few years ago."

"What?" I yelp, my voice loud enough someone bangs on the door again. "That's... I'm not *that*," I say, voice lower. I *am* a beta—a wolf incapable of siring or bearing young—but I never agreed to being a...a *molly*.

"You are if Alpha says you are," the other boy murmurs.

"Surely your pack has a ton of betas willing to…to do *that*!" I hissed. After all, most of our species were betas, as many as nine out of ten at the last census.

"It's a special job," the wolf—who must be an omega, if they hadn't had a beta in years—insists, sounding proud to be here, and I cringe at his clear naïveté. "Most of the male betas are sent to the uvite quarry, up by the old bridge, and the females serve the alphas at the packhouse, doing laundry and in the kitchens. Only the pretty ones get to live here. You should be proud."

"If it's such a *special* job, shouldn't everyone be lining up to do it?" I ask, clenching my hands into fists.

"Oh, don't worry, they do!" The omega says, his voice sounding chirpier. "But the Alphas are…discriminate. It's not often we get a beta in good enough condition to work here." He lowers his voice like he's telling me a secret, even though I don't think anyone else is listening. "My mama used to work in the kitchens and my pa, back when he was Alpha, oversaw the workers at the quarry. They were…kind. But not pretty, you know? Between the burns from the lye in the soaps and from the stove on my mama, and Pa's arthritis and bad back…" He trails off with a sigh.

"I didn't ask to be here!" I snap, resting my fist on the cold wall.

"And yet, here you are. You should be grateful," a deep voice says from behind me, and I yelp, twisting around. My heart is thudding rapidly in my chest as I slam my back into the wall, staring wide-eyed at the man who'd entered without my noticing. A quick glance at the door—if it's open, maybe I can escape—has my fear growing stronger.

He's shut it, locking me in this...this dressed-up prison cell with him. His red hair and scattering of freckles are familiar...*Dixon,* my mind dredges up—the pack Alpha, the man who stole me from the woods and locked me up.

"Just let me go," I say, aiming for a snarl. It comes out more of a whimper, weak and spineless.

"Why would I do that? We went to all this trouble to clean you up." He grins, and for the first time since waking, I realize that I'm not covered in dirt and sweat. My skin goes cold when I realize that someone had scrubbed me down. Lifting a hand to my hair, I cringe when I notice that even *it* has been washed and braided.

The realization that people had touched me in my sleep, done who knows what else, has tears stinging my eyes. "I didn't agree to this..." I whisper, rocking back on my heels and curling my arms around my knees, as if making myself small would in some way protect me.

It doesn't. The man smirks and steps closer. I bare my teeth, and he just laughs, crouching down in front of me. I kick out at him, but he grabs my ankle and gives it a yank, pulling me down until I'm flat on my back.

Too quickly for me to react, he's astride me, his weight pinning down my hips, his hands clasped around my wrists. "I'll make you a deal, little *bitch,*" Dixon says, sneering down at me, "If you can fight me off, I'll let you walk out of the door and be on your way."

I try.

I try everything I can think of—kicking, hitting, biting. Even my wolf tries to help. His claws erupt from my fingertips, and his teeth poke painfully through my gums—but I can't.

I'm not strong enough, and when it's over, he leaves me sobbing on the rug, bruised and broken.

I don't know how long I lie there before the omega in the next room speaks—long enough for my sobs to quiet and the tears to have dried itchy on my cheeks, and for the monster's seed to grow crusty on my thighs.

"Why did you fight him?" The omega's voice is soft and laced with confusion.

His naïveté does nothing but stoke my anger higher. This isn't his fault, and rationally, I know he's as much a victim as I am. More, really, since he doesn't even *know* how wrong this is.

"I'll *always* fight him," I promise hotly, to myself as much as him. I crawl closer to the loose cinderblock. "You have to know this isn't right."

"Why?" he asks. "I was born omega. This is the Goddess Moon's will."

My heart aches for him, but I set my jaw. I don't bother staying quiet when I say, "This *isn't* her will. It's...it's a *perversion*." I don't know how I know it, but I do—an innate sense of *wrong*. It's like I can hear her whispering to me.

The omega boy goes quiet.

From the other side of my cell, though, a different man speaks. The other omega's voice is sharper, less innocent. "Don't bother," he says dryly. "You'll never convince Three to disobey Alpha."

"Three?" I ask, scooting closer to the other wall to better hear.

"We don't get names. As soon as we present omega, they're taken away. He's Three. I'm Nine."

"What do the numbers mean?" I ask. I don't care, not really, but the conversation is helping draw my mind away from what just happened, the memory of the monster's hands—I shudder and pinch my thigh, careful to avoid the fingerprint-shaped bruises. The pain helps.

Nine says, "It's like…a ranking, basically. One lives with the Alpha's second-in-command as his official mate, and Two belongs to the Alpha's third. Of us here, Three is the favorite. Gets all the special treatment in exchange for being their perfect little pillow princess."

"How many of us are here?" I need to learn as much as I can about this place if I have any hope of escaping.

"You're number ten."

Chapter Six

Princeling

My headache is pounding as I stare at the young agent in rookie whites standing on the other side of my desk. No amount of rubbing my forehead chases it away, and I sigh, finally giving up and dropping my hand. "I'm sorry. I must have misunderstood, because *surely* you didn't pull me out of the field for *this*?" I wave the furled-up missive for emphasis, the red gossamer string fluttering wildly from the harsh motion. Bad enough I'd had to leave my search yesterday to come back and deal with an angry museum director, now *this*?

"I... She said it was important?" the agent answers, his voice creeping higher with every word.

I yank the string off and unravel the scroll for the second time, shoving the letter under his nose. "Tell me... Does this *look* important right now? It's an invitation...to a Faerie Ball...*next year*."

"I... Sir, she's the queen! I can't just—"

"You *can*. You're not in Faerie anymore, soldier. As far as you and this office are concerned, here in this realm she is just another stuck-up socialite with too much time and money and not enough sense. Got it?" I drop the letter into the trash, wishing I could light it on fire while I was at it.

Everyone assumed the Seelie Queen of the Summer Court to be benevolent and kind. After all, she is beautiful with her soft golden hair and skin like honey, her eyes the blue of serene waters. In this shallow world, beauty too often equated with good. It was unfair. The Unseelie King and his people had been denied the right to unrestricted travel outside of his borders, despite having been at peace for millennia.

Meanwhile, the Seelie bitch had been granted everything she'd asked for with a smile—despite her sadism, despite the bloody experiments she'd been running on *our* people for as long as she'd held the throne—simply because of her beauty. Every time I pass a mirror, I am grateful for my father, who'd looked nothing like her.

From him, I was gifted my dark skin and eyes. He had a breadth of shoulders that could put an ox to shame, or so the stories said, and I'd modeled my glamour to fit. I only wish I'd been allowed to know him. She'd turned him to stone as soon as she birthed me.

The BAA agent goes pale at the look on my face and gives a sharp nod. "Yes, Y-Your Highness."

I pinch my nose. These rookies were going to be the death of me. The poor kid had clearly just immigrated from Faerie. I could hardly blame him for a few mistakes, but clearly, the BAA training hadn't been very thorough this time around—or he just happened to be particularly dense.

"Commander," I correct, trying to keep my voice calm. "Our titles mean nothing here, young one."

"Sorry, Your—um, I mean, Commander. It won't happen again," he stutters, snapping off a quick salute.

"See that it doesn't. In the future, you would do well to treat any missive from the Queen in the same way you would one from any other species leader. Being my mother gives her no special treatment."

The young fae goes pale, likely at the thought of ignoring an order from the Queen, someone we are programmed to listen to.

"As you were," I say, sighing as I wave him out of my office. He scrambles to escape. If I didn't know better, I'd think he was worried I intended him harm, but I was careful—or thought I'd been—to avoid letting my impatience take over. I had a reputation back home, one that I'd left behind with the corpse of my last lover.

The last thing I need is for it to grow roots here.

I am no longer my mother's 'right hand'.

I've barely dropped down into my seat when my comm is going off in my ear again. *Commander Aries! Demon sighting in Midtown.*

I groan and shove myself to my feet. So much for continuing my search. "On my way," I answer, sending out a silent hope that the little wolf can hold out a bit longer.

* * * *

Daddy

My essence is leeching energy from fifteen souls when I finally have enough to risk fumbling for my bond with Eryn. It was a fledgling thing, even before we'd been separated, little more than a possibility of what *could* be. I have to hope that it is still there and strong enough that manipulating it won't cause it to shatter.

It's risky, and I know, rationally, that I should leave it alone until I've escaped, but not knowing what's happening to him is slowly torturing me. I can't even tell if he's still alive, since the damn tourmaline makes it feel like I'm wrapped in cotton, muffling my senses.

I close my eyes and reach for our bond, the gold thread that ties his soul to me, and my heart drops when I don't immediately find it. Frantically, I start to search. I've formed hundreds of bonds throughout my lifetime. Most of the bonds are dead — oily black lines leading off into nothing, the souls on the other end long since passed on. A few are sickly and faded red — old bonds I haven't tended in ages. Eventually, they too will die. Only a handful are glowing bright — the brightest is a jade cord leading home, to Maggie. Unlike the blood bonds I shared with my feeders, hers is stronger — a heart bond, formed of mutual trust from years of care.

I find all of these, and more — but no Eryn.

In my panic, I fumble around, snapping several of the old, dull bonds I'd formed with prior feeders. The sudden loss is like a missing limb — initially numb until it begins to throb, but I ignore the aching.

I can't have lost him...not here, not like this. *Not ever*, my possessive inner voice promises, but for the first time in a long time, I wonder if I can trust him.

Finally, I find it.

It's faint, barely thicker than a strand of hair, but it's *there*.

I grasp onto it carefully, feeding it energy. Slowly, it starts to pulse. I can't do much, not without Eryn with me. Already, the separation has started to fray it. If we weren't reunited in a week, two at tops, it would shatter.

A broken bond can't be reformed. Whether it flourished or withered, there's only one shot, one chance, to grow it. I *must* find him.

I feed the strand as much energy as I can spare — which isn't much, if I want my plan to work. Giving it one last, gentle stroke, I reluctantly pull away. I know now that he's alive, though I got a sense of pain and fear. I'm too weak — and the bond too muted — for me to pinpoint much else, though I did get a general sense of direction. *North...* and not far.

Soon, I send the thought down the bond, knowing he won't be able to hear it but needing to say it anyway. *Daddy's coming.*

* * * *

Pet
Sunday night

The night passes, but I don't sleep. I'm too scared of what will happen to me if I close my eyes. Staying awake doesn't help. My door is shoved open roughly regardless, revealing two wolves in human form.

A large woman and an even larger man — an alpha by his scent. The woman is a beta, I'm guessing, though she smells so strongly of bitter soap it's hard to be certain. "You. Come," the alpha grunts, snapping his fingers.

I shake my head and huddle against the bed. As much as I want out of here, the thought of going with them is paralyzing. His frown deepens, and he gives the woman a shove. "Go get him and be quick about it."

The beta's face is blank as she approaches. I don't expect her to grab me by the hair and start to drag me — she's big, but she didn't look *that* strong — so I'm unprepared when she does, yelping in pain as I try to scrabble to my feet, anything to relieve the pain on my scalp.

She gives me another good yank before shoving me toward the alpha. "Walk," she orders. "You stink of fucking. The alphas won't like it."

I don't really care whether they like it, and only the desire to feel less dirty, even if part of me feels I will never be clean again, has me reluctantly stop fighting them. They push and prod me down the hallway, finally shoving me into a large room at the end of the hall.

Immediately, I look for weak spots — a window I could break, another door, anything. There's nothing, just a cold, square room with six rusty showerheads, a drain in the center of the downward-sloped floor and four other men, all staring at me with wide, fearful eyes.

And a fifth, whose stare is sharp and calculating. Without having ever seen the man, something tells me this is Nine. Like me, and several of the other skittish boys, his skin is littered with bruises, though his range in color from yellow to purple. Unlike the rest, though, whose injuries seem limited to surface marks, his body bears layers of scars, one atop another, though none above his neck or below his elbows.

Like whoever had carved him up wanted the marks to stay covered by clothing.

Horror fills me at the sight. I've seen wolves in my pack lose entire limbs to bear traps and regrow them on the next Goddess Moon. The only time a were would scar was if the wound was packed with wolfsbane and silver. Whoever gave him those marks didn't want them to heal.

I must stare too long, because Nine bares his teeth at me before turning his back, and the beta behind me shoves me forward. "Go clean yourself, but best be quick. Showers shut off in ten minutes."

I scurry to the last empty showerhead, right next to Nine, wincing when I step under the sputtering stream of icy water. He glares at me until I hunch my shoulders, turning my face away quickly.

There's a little shelf in front of me, but the only thing on it is a bar of cheap-looking, off-white soap. The only thing worse than a cold shower would be it cutting off halfway through, so I grab the bar quickly and start to lather it up. I clean my body, careful to get every nook and cranny, hissing as I clean my tender hole. I don't dare to be as thorough as I want to be, though, the stinging pain forestalling me.

Then, I get my hands covered in as much foam as I can before replacing the bar on the shelf. I start working the harsh soap through my long hair. Without conditioner or oil, I know it will be a knotted mess when I'm finished, and part of me hopes for it.

I've always known my hair is my best feature. Even my mother, who'd hated me, had refused to cut it. I can still remember the moments between her rages when she'd pet it softly, her fingers gentle for the first and only time.

If my hair is tangled and ruined, will they still want me here, or would they send me to the quarry? Would I have an easier time escaping from there?

"Two minutes!" the beta barks, so I hurriedly hold my hair under the water, soap spilling down to the tiles as I try to rinse it. Goosebumps rise on my skin, and I start to shiver, my teeth chattering.

As soon as I'm clean, I hurry out of the water, careful not to slip on the wet tile floor, and wrap my arms around my hunched chest. "A-are there t-towels?" I ask the beta, my voice loud in the room that is otherwise silent, except for the sound of showering.

"No talking!" the beta orders, her face stoney.

I go silent, but another voice speaks up. Nine steps out of his shower and shakes his head, water flying everywhere, then says, "Only good boys get towels. Unlike *them*" — he angles his head at the other omegas, who all seem careful to be quiet and obedient, cringing away from him,

even if it puts them farther under the icy spray — "I'm not bending over nicely just to get a scrap of sandpaper to rub my balls with."

I can't help it. His snide comments and the look on his face draw a snicker out of my mouth, a sound I never thought I'd make in this hellhole. The beta seems less amused, though, as her hand drops to her waist, landing on the grip of a furled whip at her side that I'm just now noticing.

I stumble back a step, but Nine stays planted, just…looking at her, almost as if he's daring her to do it. Instead, she grits her teeth, then says, "Line up."

As if the words were a signal, the showerheads sputter and the water is cut off. There's an awkward shuffle as we form an uneven line, all of us except for

Nine, who stalls long enough that the beta lurches toward him. Only then does the omega step calmly into line behind me.

I want to be him when I grow up, I think, awed by his bravery as we're prodded out of the room and back to our cells.

Chapter Seven

Pet
Monday afternoon

"What is this mess?" Dixon grabs my hair, which had indeed dried to a tangled mess, and yanks hard enough that I cry out.

"It's not my fault," I yelp, though inwardly, I know I didn't do anything to prevent it. At the time, the little rebellion had felt justified. I'd been *proud* of it, but now, facing the consequences, all I feel is fear.

"Are you implying it's mine?" he asks, eyes narrowed to slits and real anger flashing on his face.

I shake my head, at least as much as I can with his tight grip still fisted in my hair. "No! No, just...the soap. It's not good for it. I'm sorry!" The worst part about the apology is knowing that I mean it. I might have felt good about it then, in the showers, but that feeling is gone now. Now, I'm so terrified that my bladder is threatening to release, snot is pouring like a faucet from my nose and tears sting my eyes.

I don't know whether it's how miserable I look or that the argument actually makes sense, because some of his anger seems to dim, his snarl replaced with a frown. "Hmm. Well, I suppose such a delicate thing might need more care..." He softens his grip until it turns more to a caress, and I barely hold back my shudder.

Abruptly, he releases me, letting me fall to the carpet, then strides for the door. He raps on it and one of the guard's peers through the window before letting him out.

I draw in a shaky breath then wipe my face in my hands. I want to curse or scream but it won't do any good, just have the guards banging at the door. I'm considering crawling into the bed when the door opens again and I flinch, my heart pounding, before I realize it's not Dixon, or another alpha, but a slim-framed male with large gold eyes and a smile that looks too genuine to be fake.

"Hello," he says, and I recognize his voice immediately as the omega from the cell next to me, the one Nine had named Three. He wasn't one of the boys who'd showered with me this morning. After a second, his face falls, his smile slipping off. "Oh, dear. I see what he means."

"What—?" I start to say, but then he moves toward me, the door closing behind him, and I see the small blue bag in his hand. I can't tell everything it holds, but a fancy curved hairbrush is peeking from the partially opened zipper.

"Alpha sent me to help you. He even gave me permission to use my *detangler*," Three says, enough awe in the last word that I know it's considered a luxury here. So far, all the omegas I've seen have hair that is at least as long as their shoulders. I wince at the thought of trying to keep it neat without some form of product. Three's hair is longer than any of the others, though not quite as long as mine. And where mine is pale blond, his is a pretty nutmeg brown, shiny and healthy.

He sits crisscross in front of me, seeming completely unaware, or at least unworried, about his nudity or mine, and starts to carefully empty his little bag. A brush, two combs, a little tub of hair cream and a fancy spray bottle. He even has a hair tie.

"Turn around?" he asks, and I hate to think it, but I can see why he's the favorite, with his soft hands and angelic voice. I want to be angry at him. Nine told me last night that they don't even lock him in. He could leave at any time, let any of *us* out at any time, but he's so brainwashed, he would never do it. So, I *want* to hate him, to lump him in with our captors in my head, but I can't.

What terrible things has he seen, have been done *to* him, to make him like this? Either he's grown up never knowing different, which isn't his fault, or they've broken him into this, which *still* isn't his fault.

So, without protest, I obediently scoot around, giving him my back and letting him work his magic. First, he sprays the detangler along the strands. He is gentle as he starts to work out the knots, first with his fingers, then with the comb. Finally, he is able to run the brush smoothly through it. I think he's done, but then he grabs the little tub of cream, working it through as well. I find myself relaxing for the first time since waking up here, lulled into a stupor by his efforts.

"May I braid it?" he asks, finally breaking the silence.

"Okay," I answer, my voice small, and he hums, meticulously separating my hair into sections with nimble fingers, starting at the top of my head.

KD Ellis

I don't think he's going to say anything else, but then he surprises me. His voice is little more than a whisper when he asks, "What was your pack like?"

I take a second to gather my thoughts. Do I tell him about being lonely? About never fitting in? About the teasing and the bullying and never feeling fully at home?

In the end, I decide to concentrate on the good things. Maybe, if he sees that this is wrong, that there are other places, other *choices*, he'll start to realize that he deserves more than this. That an alpha doesn't love you just because he gives you a towel and conditioner before he ruts you.

I talk to him about the field of lilies I used to visit every spring, and the garden our pack tended year-round. So far, the amount of dry, partly rancid meat we'd been fed has me suspecting that vegetables are rare here, likely saved for the alphas.

I tell him about the blanket that Crazy Pat crocheted for me when I was ten. It had been pink and frogged, and Pat never remembered anyone's name, so she'd embroidered it with 'Ellen', but it had been soft and warm.

"What about your Alpha?" Three's fingers are moving slowly now, like he's taking his time, like he's so enthralled with my stories, he's forgotten the reason he is here in the first place.

"Our Alpha? He was…nice. For a while, he was like a father to me, when I was little, but" — I sigh and shrug my shoulder — "I grew up. Things changed."

"Did he not like you anymore because you got too old for him?" Three asks, and his voice is so quiet I almost can't hear him. For the first time, his fingers get too tight in my hair, pulling painfully at my scalp.

I yelp, and immediately, he lets go like he's been burned, stammering an apology that I wave off. "No, it wasn't like that," I say, wondering how to word it. "The Alpha of my pack was a good man. He didn't do...*this*." I wave at the prison I've been trapped in. "Our omegas are free to live in the pack just like all the other betas and alphas do. And mating is something people do by choice. No one is forced to just because of their designation."

"I don't understand," Three murmurs, but he lifts his hands back to my hair and continues braiding. "Alpha says that not all packs are like this. That...that the *other* packs don't keep their omegas safe like we do. That...that they just stay in the village and anyone who wants them can just take them at will. That you just get used *over* and *over* and *over*, and they don't even give you a break there. They just line up, one after another. Alpha says I should be grateful, because he only lets me be used twice a day."

My heart breaks for him. He's not much older than me but he sounds younger—like a lost boy. "Other packs don't let their omegas get 'used' at all. They have a choice. They can say 'no'."

Three goes silent for a long moment, then roughly ties off my braid as he jerks to his feet. "I...I don't believe you." By the time I turn around, he's at the door and a guard is letting him out. He leaves without looking back, and my stomach turns to a rock.

I'd hoped...

Well. It doesn't matter now.

* * * *

Princeling

"What did it take?" I ask one of the agents on site as we pick our way through the rubble. The Rubin

Museum of Art had suffered more damage than the last handful that had been hit, but it was a careless sort — like the Whisper had thrown a tantrum in the middle of the heist.

"It's hard to say for sure with all the destruction it caused, but the cameras picked it up initially in the geology section. Our guess is one of the gemstones, but the museum staff hasn't been allowed in to start cataloging yet," Agent Mick explains. He looks a bit shellshocked as he clambers over a fallen antique column. I can't blame him too much. The damage is excessive, even for a demon.

And methodical. The way the shattered glass is splayed on the tiles is hauntingly beautiful — almost like art itself.

"Why not?" I ask, pausing near a cracked clay bust. It's vital that we know exactly what has gone missing from each site if we hope to figure out what it's after, especially if we hope to stop it before it enacts whatever it's planning. So far, we haven't found a connection.

An Egyptian arched harp circa 1300 B.C. taken from the Met, a Chinese ji traced back to the Zhou dynasty and even, odd though it was, the taxidermized carcass of an Indonesian peafowl. We had our historians combing through historical text for any similarities between their history, but so far, no luck.

"The place was quiet when we got here," Agent Mick says, jarring me from my thoughts, and it takes me a second to realize he's answering my question, "but we can't spot the demon leaving on any of the cameras."

I freeze in place and stare at him in horror. "If the Whisper is still *here,* then why are we?" Dozens of techs are combing the wreckage, all unarmed, and I can see from where I'm standing at least as many agents strolling casually through the halls, cataloging the damage and hardly paying attention to their surroundings, much like Agent Mick and I had been doing.

"We combed the place twice, Boss. There's no sign of it," Agent Mick promises, and I sigh.

"Gods save us from fools," I mutter to the ceiling, then reach for my radio. "Be advised, there—"

I don't get to finish my warning. Suddenly, the ceiling tiles above us seem to explode, sending white powder and chunks of plaster down on us like rain, and a heavy weight lands on my chest, knocking me flat on my back on the tiles. I feel the broken glass pierce my nape and arms along the edge of my Kevlar vest, but the pain doesn't have time to register before adrenaline kicks in.

I go to attack, but the Whisper is quick...too quick. Its razor-sharp claws clamp around my windpipe, piercing my skin. I feel my warm blood start to bead up, not quick enough to be deadly—but that could change at any moment.

"Move and I kill him," the Whisper snarls, eyeing the frozen agents that surround us. "Tell them to leave," it orders me, though it refuses to meet my gaze. It's smart enough to know better.

I swallow down my fear and try to talk through its tight grip. "Fall back," I order, and my men hesitate before they obediently start their retreat. The Whisper doesn't move until we are alone in the gallery. I hear my men muttering in the hall, likely preparing to attack, but they are out of sight.

The Whisper finally looks down at me. I feel the heavy weight of its mind pressing against mine. I struggle to shield my mind, but it's a skill I haven't practiced since I left Faerie behind. I'm not strong enough to keep it out completely.

"You are friendssss with my prince," it hisses.

"Yes," I bark out an answer, not bothering to lie. In the seconds it took me to protect my mind, it had likely already seen what it wanted.

"Passss him a messssage. Tell him—" the Whisper starts to say something, but then the black collar around its throat seems to pulse. It hisses, its head snapping to the side and teeth grinding, until the band settles. "Cursssse thissss world, and itssss *magic*." It spits the last word like a jinx, tiny nose scrunching, then looks back at me. "My masssster's plan is clossssse. His weapon is—" Again, the collar spasms, and again the Whisper curses.

Its fingers loosen around my neck, just enough I can draw in a breath to ask, "Weapon? Is there anything you can tell me about it?" I almost feel bad for it. Whispers rarely came to earth—and never legally. The few who tried to apply for a visa were denied on sight. Like Bloodwraiths, they were simply too deadly and unpredictable to risk.

Whispers though, unlike Bloodwraiths, rarely bothered to apply. I'd asked Levi why once, after hearing about the trouble S.T.A.R.S. was having hunting one down over in Europe, and he'd said that there was nothing here for them. Unlike other demons, they didn't feed on blood or fear or lust. They feed on silence, something Levi claimed was hard to find up here. He'd said that most who ended up here did so because they were summoned, not by choice—and the resulting chaos of noise drove them insane.

This one seems to have acclimated well enough, perhaps due to the collar clasped around its throat.

Whatever the reason, I regret its inevitable fate. It seems like it wishes to help.

"Very little," it answers. "Thissss," it scratches at the black band on its throat, "is already calling me back. But if my massssster suceeedssss, the balance will fail. Tell him... Tell him to remember Tripper."

"Tripper? Who is—?" I try to ask, but the Whisper just snarls, then it is gone—as if it was never there in the first place. I draw in a ragged breath and sit up, carefully scanning the area. I release it in a shock of relief, placing a hand to my chest to steady my beating heart before I call my men back in.

They rush through the doors like a stampede. "It's gone," I say without preamble, accepting Agent Mick's extended hand to help me up. "Find out what's missing and let me know immediately. I need to speak to Leviathan."

"Good luck," he calls after me, the words fading behind me as I step onto the sidewalk.

Chapter Eight

Pet

I don't need a calendar or a clock to realize what day it is. As the sun sets, the Goddess Moon starts to call for me. Her voice is sandpaper to my skin but somehow also a warm blanket, soothing away the chill of the room. A threat and a promise at the same time, and I don't know what to feel, what to believe.

I can almost hear her voice, promising that *this* month it will be different. But like a battered wife, I cringe away from her platitudes, unable to trust the hand that has struck me down so many times.

Inside me, my wolf whines, and I realize I've never felt so close to him. For the first time in my life, I don't see him as my enemy, though I'm not sure I trust him enough to call him a friend.

He rubs his muzzle against my ribs in comfort, and I sink into the feeling, until my cell door opens abruptly, chasing it away.

Dixon struts in, kicking the door closed behind him, and I cringe away from him, huddling against the side of the bed like I think that will in some way protect me. I try to lower my eyes, but this close to the Goddess Moon, my wolf is nearing the surface and he refuses to let me.

Dixon pauses, staring at me curiously. I expect anger and violence, but he seems amused more than anything. "I hear you've been telling stories," he finally says.

"Nothing that isn't the truth," I whisper back, wishing my voice was stronger—wishing *I* were stronger.

"Well, I hope you're happy. I sent Three in here to help fix you up, and you repaid him with a truth he didn't ask for. He was happy, you know, believing this was best for him, that we were just protecting him from the big bad wolves." Dixon curls his fingers in the air like quotation marks as he says the last few words.

"But it wasn't true," I argue. "You lied to him."

"But he was happy. Do you feel better knowing he cried today?" Dixon arches a brow, but he's smiling, like *he* doesn't care. "I had to beat him. It's been years since he's needed a lashing. I should thank you. I forgot how much I missed his tears."

I cringe even more, clapping a hand over my mouth. I didn't want the omega to get hurt, never that. I just wanted him to...

To what? To sneak out of his cell and let you free, then you could all run away together into the night? My inner voice is snarky as it derides me for being a fool. Even if the poor boy *had* snuck out, and even if I *had* convinced him to let us all free, how had I thought it was going to work? Ten wolves running aimlessly through the woods, no direction, nowhere to go... What had I expected? A happy-ever-after? This isn't a fairytale or a story book.

"Consider this a show of my gratitude." Dixon grins, chucking a tube of something toward me. It rolls along the floor, coming to a stop against my bare foot, and all it takes is a look at the label for tears to burn my eyes. I don't feel grateful—or to be more honest, I don't *want* to feel grateful—and I hate myself because I *do*. It's a tube of lube with the plastic wrapper still around the cap.

"And," he adds as he heads back toward the door, "you'll be happy to know, I'm giving you *all* the night off. Now that there's no reason for my men and I to play nice, we showed your little friend exactly what he's been missing. Go ahead and enjoy the break, bitch. It'll be the last quiet night you'll get until the next Goddess Moon." He waggles his fingers at me as he slams the door behind him.

I don't know if it's because of his haste to leave, or that the door malfunctions or if it's Goddess Moon looking out for me, but my breath catches in my throat as I watch the door close...then bounce back open before the lock can catch.

Quickly, before any of the guards can notice, I grab the pillow off my bed and strip it naked, then scramble across the floor to the door. "Please work, *please*," I pray as I shove the fabric of the pillowcase into the locking mechanism in the doorframe, then carefully, heart pounding, push the door close. It sticks and I wait, fearing I'll hear the lock engage...but it *doesn't*.

Hope soars.

If the guards join the pack run, and it sounds like they might, if I'm understanding Dixon's threat correctly, then tonight could be the only chance we get. I just have to convince the others to leave with me.

I draw in a steadying breath, trying to communicate with my inner wolf. I need him to work with me, tonight more than ever. If he can keep from taking over *just* until we get free, we might have a chance.

Then, we just need to figure out where to go.

My wolf chimes in with something that feels like a promise, then whispers, *home-not-home. We go to Not Alpha.*

It takes me a long second for it to click. "*Home-not-home, Not Alpha…*"

He wants us to go back to my pack.

My heart drops as I realize we have no choice. We can't go back to Old York, not with Puck running free and still searching for us, and we can't make it all the way to Brekkan, not on foot, and definitely not with the whole Brooklyn Pack on our tails.

But my old pack lived in the forest outside of New Havenwood, which isn't that far.

Can you find it? I ask him, fear mingling with hope. If we can get there, they'll protect the omegas, I know they will. They just won't protect *me*.

Yes.

It's decided.

As soon as the halls are clear…we're going home.

* * * *

Daddy

Forty-seven.

I have forty-seven links formed when my cell shivers. It's subtle at first, and I almost miss it, but the second time is stronger. I flatten my palms on the floor as everything starts to move — lifting, as if I were lying on the bottom of an old elevator rising up the shaft, out of a basement.

It's been decades since I helped with the blueprints, and I'd almost forgotten about this. The prisoners kept here were too dangerous to risk opening the doors to speak to them after the initial binding agent wears off. They opened only to bring prisoners in or out.

More often than not, they are only ever opened once.

When the guards wished to speak to the inmates, they used an intercom spell. And during trials, the prisoners stayed in the cells. The cells were just brought to the judge.

A small part of me is curious to see who wants to speak to me now. The larger part of me doesn't care. Too much of my attention is taken up with holding the links together, siphoning off the energy as quickly but carefully as possible. I can't risk leakage, not when I only have one shot at this. And if they break too soon, I won't have enough energy to blast through the wards.

It feels like trying to perform surgery when all I have is a spoon and rusty garden shears.

The feeling of moving is disorienting. Intentionally so, meant to give the illusion of twists and turns that didn't exist to keep the prisoner confused. A confused prisoner is a calm one — or a calmer one, anyway.

It had been past the idea of past me, *present* me hated myself for thinking of it. By the time my cell stops moving, I feel dizzy, nauseous, and completely unprepared for the small window that appears in the wall. It's not, unfortunately, a weakness I can exploit. It's made of magically charged crystals that only activate when lined up with another set of *equally* charged crystals. Once activated, they formed a one-way mirror of sorts.

People outside could see in, but the inmate only sees a blank white square. Sound could travel both ways, allowing those outside to communicate with the one inside. *Also my idea.* It kept inmates from seeing who they spoke to, and that anonymity was another layer of protection for the witnesses, lawyers, *whoever* was on the other side. In the unlikely event a prisoner *did* manage to escape, they wouldn't have a target to blame for their incarceration.

They couldn't kill someone they couldn't find, after all, and even the best trackers needed to know *who* the target was to locate them.

Most of the time, anyway.

It doesn't work as well when the person on the other side is someone they know. I don't need to see Aries to recognize his voice when he starts to speak. "Levi? Can you hear me?"

I set my jaw and turn my face away from the crystals. Unless he's here to apologize and let me out — *doubtful* — then nothing he has to say is worth me getting distracted.

I hear his sigh come through, then he starts speaking again. "It's fine. You don't have to look at me. Just...listen, okay?" He pauses again, like he thinks *now* I'm going to say something. "Does the name Tripper mean anything to you?"

"It's not a name," I blurt, the shock of hearing the word drawing the words out of me without warning.

"Then what is it?" Aries asks.

I close my eyes, torn. The angry part of me wants to stay silent, let him suffer the way *I'm* suffering. The rational part hesitates. What if I stay silent but an answer could have led them to Puck? To *Eryn?*

"It's not a name, it's a place. Three cities who defected from the rule of the Nameless One and were dest— Wait," I frown and finally turn toward the crystals. "How did you hear of it? It happened millennia before *your* world was formed, let alone *this* one."

"Ran into the Whisper. You were right. It's been collared for sure. It said to remind you of Tripper."

"*Tripeur,*" I correct as I close my eyes, trying to think about why the Whisper would want me to remember something I had barely been alive for. I was still an imp then, barely hatched. I remember my father being stressed and people yelling all the time, but honestly, that describes pretty much my whole childhood.

"Think, Levi," I mutter to myself, ignoring Aries rattling on about something. Stories of the Calamity were like bedtime stories for young imps now — but like all bedtime stories, they'd been grossly exaggerated.

Three cities ruled by three demon brothers who were unhappy with the way the Nameless One was running Kur. They'd gathered their supporters and fled to a sprawling network of caves near the Abyss.

" —vi. Leviathan." Aries snaps my name loud, like it's not the first time he's said it. When I look toward the crystals again, he asks, "Why did the Whisper want you to remember three dead cities?"

I shake my head, honestly not certain. "I don't know. It's a *bedtime* story. Barely anyone even believes that the cities were *real,* Aries!" I know I sound frustrated, but this feels like a waste of time — a distraction, to keep us from looking into the *real* plan. "The Whisper had to have said something else."

"Just that Puck's plan is nearly complete. It said that if he succeeds, the balance will fail, and something about a weapon," Aries answers, and he sounds as exasperated as I feel.

"Weapon?" I bark, the word clicking in my head. "Hang on. What's been stolen so far?"

Aries starts listing, "An Egyptian was-scepter, circa 2900 BC. A Greek psalterion—I think it's a type of harp?—circa 300 BC. A second harp, this one Egyptian. A taxidermy corpse of an Indonesian peafowl from just before the species went extinct. There was…an obsidian arrowhead found in an old Aztec burial site, and a Chinese ji. Then there was the labradorite pendant of Princess Nata—"

With each item, a sense of dread builds in my chest. He's still speaking when I interrupt him. "He's building an Astra."

Chapter Nine

Pet

Run. Run now, my wolf urges, pacing back and forth inside my chest.

"Wait," I murmur back, pressing my palm against my sternum. "Not yet."

Now, he howls, and fur bristles along my elbows until I grit my teeth, forcing back the change.

"Wait," I say again, a bit louder — a bit more dominant. I still hear laughter on the other end of the hall, outside my cell. Clearly, a few alphas are still lingering, taking their time as they steal their pleasure from the cloistered omegas. It seems to take forever before I hear the loud thud of a heavy door closing, then the softer click of it latching. I wait to hear a lock, but they must think the locks on our cells are enough of a precaution.

To be fair, I already hear broken cries somewhere nearby as the Goddess Moon starts to whisper, drawing someone into an early shift. Once shifted, they wouldn't even need to lock us in. Without opposable thumbs, the doors are basically impenetrable anyway.

Now. Now. Now, my wolf demands, and I finally give in.

I pull open the door.

The hallway is eerie. The guards had shut off most of the lights, leaving it dark but for the running lamps along the bottom of the walls, and the only sounds are the panting and howling of the early shifters, begging to be released. I hesitate but turn to the left first.

Stretching up on my tiptoes, I peer into Nine's cell. He's still human, mostly, pacing near the far wall. "*Psst,*" I hiss, holding my breath until he looks at me. His eyes are glowing. Clearly, he is fighting against the shift—and losing.

"Ten? How did you—?" His words are guttural, but I cut him off before he can finish.

"No time… We need to hurry. I'm opening the door. Will you help me get the rest out?" I grab the door handle, grateful that the alphas were so worried about getting into the cells quickly that they settled for what amounts to a childproof lock—latched from the inside but easy to open from the out. All I need to do is fumble with a little button and the door handle turns.

In seconds, Nine is standing right in front of me, his hands fisting and unclenching, over and over. Clearly, the Goddess Moon is calling him even more strongly than me. "Not all of them will leave with us," Nine warns.

I frown, but I know he's right. "I won't force them to. The best I can do is unlock their doors. What they do after that is up to them."

Nine sighs as I start unlatching each, yanking the cell doors open quickly before moving from one to the next. Nine grabs my hand when I go to unlock Three's.

"Don't be stupid. He'll betray us. You should leave him," Nine cautions.

"If I was being smart, I'd have left all of you," I tell him, yanking my hand free and unlocking the door. "I think you'll be surprised."

Three is huddled on his bed—an ornate, four-poster with silk sheets that had likely been expensive, once. Now, they are rumpled and dirty, covered in suspicious white patches and blood.

Three is unrecognizable. His injuries don't look life threatening, at least, but his face is swollen, his naked body more black-and-blue than unmarked flesh.

"Shit," Nine breathes, sounding as shocked as I feel. I'd had to hear it. I'd *known* what was happening, thanks to that fucker Dixon, but seeing it... I hadn't really understood.

I rush inside, my hand hovering over one of the few unmarked patches of skin for a second before I gently shake him. "Three? Three, come on. We're gonna get you out of here. You gotta stand up, okay?"

Three curls tighter into a ball. Nine rushes over and grabs my shoulder. "Come on. We have to go. Just leave him."

"If you're so worried, then leave. But I'm not leaving him behind. This is my fault." I grit my teeth and make a decision. I may be small and weak...but Three is even smaller than I am.

As carefully as I can, I slide my arms under his knees and shoulders, breathing out as I lift him. He's heavy but manageable, though guilt swarms me as he lets out what is obviously a pained moan.

I hope that once we are out of this place, under the light of the Goddess Moon, he'll shift. As broken as he is, it will hurt, but the injuries will be healed.

Nine sighs but holds the door for me, then moves to unlock the last one. By the time we're headed for the exterior door, there's five of us.

Only two others have decided to take the risk. Eight has already shifted. He's a brindled wolf, too skinny for his size. He's hovering by my knees, his tail tucked and ears laid flat. Five is still human, though fur coats the back of his forearms and elbows.

Nine glances at me, then at the other omegas. "You sure about this? Once we're out, there's no going back."

The wolf gives a little yip, dipping his chin in a facsimile of a nod.

"Open the door," I say.

His fingers flex on the knob. "Just outside, there's a ten-foot clear space, then there's the woods. If we're lucky, the pack is still on the other side of the village. If they aren't, we're going to have to run fast."

"Try to keep northeast," I add. "We're heading toward my...the Havenwood Pack. We'll be safe there."

"I thought we'd be safe here," the other omega says. I don't recognize him.

"It'll be different there, I promise." They might be small-minded sometimes, and I might never have fit in, but they aren't malicious. Even Beta had looked out for me, in his own way. The Flesh Market may have been more deadly than he'd implied, but it wasn't a tribunal of elders, or worse—the Lycan Council.

I drag in a breath. "Nine, it's time. Open the door."

* * * *

Princeling

"An Astra? I've never heard of it," I say, leaning closer to the crystal window to stare down at my best friend. For a second, I waver, wondering if I can trust anything he's saying.

Would he steer me wrong out of spite?

No, I decide, he wouldn't, not when Eryn is still out there. Not when one wrong step could be the difference between recovering him safe and recovering his body.

Levi looks uncomfortable as he finally twists his head to face me. His skin is bone pale, more so than usual, even, and his eyes look glassy, like a drunkard after another shot of vodka.

"Are you...feeling okay?" I ask, hesitating to continue my interrogation. I can't let him out, not even if he *is* sick, but we can get a medic to port in a palliative.

Levi bares his teeth. "Never better," he grits out, and I don't think it's my imagination that his canines look...sharper.

I swallow my discomfort and continue on, even as unease swirls in my belly. A cold breeze snakes along the nape of my neck. "What's an Astra?"

"The Destroyer," Levi says, voice tight, and he turns his face away. "The World Ender. A weapon the likes of which hasn't been seen on this planet since its birth."

"How do we stop it?"

"You don't," he says—and he looks back at me, staring directly at the crystal window. His eyes are living rubies, glowing bright.

"Well, shit."

Chapter Ten

Princeling

"They shouldn't be doing that," I mutter to the analyst standing beside me. Both of us are staring down at Leviathan. Or, more accurately, at his glowing scarlet eyes. "Right? That's not...normal?"

I've muted the comms. As far as my friend is concerned, I left a few minutes ago to track down information on the Astra.

To be fair, I do have several *other* analysts scouring the archives for references to it. I even had an envoy traveling to Kur in hopes that someone there would have any information. But I hadn't left, not yet.

"Bloodwraith, you say?" The analyst, a Cyclopies, scratches his eyebrow as he peers down. "It is...*unusual* but not unheard of. The tourmaline is likely interacting with his aura. I wouldn't be too concerned."

"You're certain?" I ask, because I'm *not* certain. I know Levi too well and have known him for too *long* to think he's not plotting something.

The analyst huffs and heads toward the door. "Nothing is *certain*. There are only scales of probability. It is *improbable* that he will escape. Now, may I be excused? I have work to get back to."

I wave him away, then stare down at Levi for a few moments longer. He certainly doesn't *look* like he's up to anything. I don't trust it.

Unfortunately, I don't have a choice. There's no evidence to prove otherwise, and until he actually tries something, there's nothing to go on, no way to guess his plan. I sigh and leave the observatory.

Almost immediately, my comm starts buzzing in my ear. I take a second to breathe through my immediately rising stress levels, then thumb the button. "Sit rep?"

"Report of a Whisper sighting on Long Island, down near that warehouse that burned down a few days ago. We sent a team door to door. No luck, but one of the residents at the apartment complex across the street is asking for you." Agent Mick says immediately.

"How'd the witness get my name?" I immediately ask as I start for the stairs.

"One of the rookies must have let it slip. Honestly, Boss? I think it's just a looky-loo," Agent Mick adds the last in a tone of voice that clearly reveals his exasperation.

"Any sign of occult activity in the home?" I ask, running my fingers over my toolbelt as I wait for a reply. I don't want to ignore a solid lead, but I can't waste time chasing ghosts, either.

"Just the standard stuff for a practitioner. A few newer copies of the Necronomicon, some tallow candles. We didn't get to look much beyond the sitting room, though, Boss. Still, kid's right creepy, though.

Gives me the willies." I can hear the unquiet in Agent Mick's voice.

"Great. *So* glad you name-dropped me." I sigh as I reach the barracks and start gearing up again. "Give me twenty."

I end the comm call, grab my jacket then stride down the hall and downstairs. I leave headquarters without looking back. Twenty minutes was an optimistic ETA, and I'll need every minute if I want to be on time.

* * * *

I don't make it on time.

An extra ten minutes isn't much in the grand scheme of things, but when I park my bike at the curb outside the three-story apartment complex, my men are standing on the sidewalk, visibly uncomfortable.

When I join them, I can tell why.

"Is that sulfur?" I ask, wrinkling my nose at the stench as soon as I pull off my helmet.

"Boss, I've smelled sulfur a *lot* in the past few months, but it's never reeked *this* bad," Agent Mick answers through the blue-and-white-patterned bandana he's got tied around his face.

It's a good idea. If only I were dressed in my usual fare, I could pull out my linen handkerchief and do the same, but I didn't think to bring it when I changed into tactical gear.

"It's not coming from the apartment," I decide after taking a brief walk around the outside. The closer I get to the street, the stronger the stench grows. I nod toward the warehouse. "You had a team comb through it already?"

Agent Mick joins me at the street, his right hand resting on the hilt of his silver dagger, like he was expecting the Whisper to jump out at any moment. I felt more comfortable immediately, having him at my side. He was small for a dhampir, but there were few others I trusted to have my back in a fight. "They did a quick look through for bodies immediately after the fire, and our team did a more thorough one when we got here, but we're still waiting on the fire marshal to release the property. There's too much underlying foundational and structural damage to go in now."

"I want the arson report on my desk as soon as it's finished," I say, finally turning my back on the ruined building.

"You think it's connected, too, don't you?" Agent Mick follows me toward the front door of the apartment.

"I'd say it's probable. Why else would the Whisper be lingering around?" I answer. Inwardly, though, I can't help thinking, *And why did it allow itself to be spotted?* The damn demon had been evading us easily this whole time. Fuck, I'd been in the same damn room with it and hadn't even noticed. Then all of a sudden, it decides to skip down the sidewalk, teeth on full display?

No, it *wanted* us to know it was here. Now we just needed to find out why.

"Who knows? Why does a Whisper do *anything*?" Agent Mick shudders as he says it but straightens up when I put my hand on the door handle. "You want me to go in with you, Boss?"

I think about it for a moment before I shake my head. "Pick two men to stay with me, then take the rest back to headquarters. Leave us the smaller sedan."

Agent Mick gives me a salute before he turns sharply on his heel, pointing at two men in rapid succession.

Good picks, I think, nodding my head toward the two agents. Both are young—though everyone is these days, compared to me—but have enough experience under their belt to be helpful in a fight.

Not that I'm expecting one, but I find it's better to prepare for an unlikely battle that doesn't happen than to be *unprepared* for one that does.

"What apartment?" I ask Agent White as the rest of the team heads back to the tactical vehicle parked at the corner.

The selkie snaps to attention. "Three-o-one, Commander Aries. Top floor, end of the hall. He has a red door." His voice is raspy, as if he spent all weekend at a concert, and I make note to have Agent Mick send him to the sea soon. My men have been pushing themselves too hard, between tracking down the portals and chasing the Whisper all across town.

We head upstairs. I avoid the elevator, since the rickety thing looks one trip away from falling into the basement, but the stairs don't look much better. They bow under our weight, creaking ominously.

With every step, I expect one to break and send us tumbling to a lower floor, but we make it safely, if a bit shakily, to the third-floor landing. "Jesus, how old is this place?" I mutter, staring at the orange and black diamond patterned carpet.

"The Westbrook Apartment Complex was built in 2172 by an architect named Ju—" Agent Essex starts to answer, his thin mane twitching, before I wave my hand. He's a living encyclopedia, as his kind is known to be. I can't hold it against him. It goes against a

Sphinx's nature *not* to answer questions. They're too much like riddles, from what I've gathered.

His skin turns pink and his tail twitches before he tucks it into his belt loop. "Sorry, Commander."

"No need to apologize." Feeling a bit guilty, I offer him a bit of busy work. Hopefully, it will forestall the side effects of an unanswered question. Normally, I'm better at remembering not to ask them off hand around him. It's been a hectic month. "When we get back, will you write up a report on the building and leave it on my desk? The history may end up important to our investigation."

Immediately, Agent Essex brightens. "Yes, Commander."

"Good man," I praise, then start down the hallway toward the red door. The *only* red door, I notice as we pass the rest. All the rest are off-white to gray, like decades of dirt have layered atop each other to create a new, mottled surface. The walls are the same. What was likely once a vibrant orange is nearing tan now. Handprints are clearly visible in places, one stacked over another, like generations of people have run their palms along the same places.

In this neighborhood, likely they have.

The red door opens before we reach it, but no one is there. A chill crowds the hallway, shivering and thick — like an invisible presence, waiting…watching.

"Well, *that's* not creepy at all," Agent White mutters under his breath. I frown at him for breaking protocol — there are plenty of unseen creatures in the world, any one of whom could have just taken offense — but inwardly, I can't help but agree with him. "Sorry, Commander," he apologizes, and I accept it with a nod.

"Agent White, I want you to stay in the hallway. Keep an eye out and your comm line open. Agent Essex, you're with me." Orders given, I take a steadying breath, realizing for the first time since we entered that the stench of sulfur is entirely missing.

An apartment complex this old and this rundown could never have a filtering system good enough to make a dent in the smell, so it must be magic. Goosebumps raise the hairs on my arms. Whoever we are going to see is the real deal — not just a dabbler but a practitioner, and a strong one, to run a spell like *that*.

Well.

This is going to be fun.

Chapter Eleven

Princeling

"Hello?" I call from the doorway, leaning forward as I try to look around without crossing the threshold. Everything looks...boring, actually. From the tone of Agent Mick's voice on the comm, I expected it to look like an occult shop—particularly like one of the over-the-top occult shops run by frauds hoping to trick tourists into buying tarot cards that never worked and Ouija boards that *did*.

Fucking Ouija boards.

Don't get me wrong. There's definitely an altar straight across from the door, next to the archway that leads deeper into the apartment, but there's nothing alarming on it—no animal skeletons or voodoo dolls to speak of. There were just four candles—all different colors, one on each corner of the knee-high wooden bench, a toning bowl in the center, surrounded by various other Wiccan elements.

Three acorns next to a stone bowl filled with clear water, a half-rotted apple next to a fresh one... A bundle of dried herbs—my guess, from the smell, is alder and angelica, mixed with a bit of bay leaf.

Unless this altar is a front—and it seems too well-loved, the instruments worn but cared for, to believe that—whatever practitioner lives in this apartment is not one who dabbles in the Dark Arts.

"Come inside, Commander Aries. Bring young Agent Essex with you," a voice calls from inside, masculine but soft, I notice, before I freeze. It's possible that my name he could have gathered from whatever rookie interviewed him, but how did he know Essex's? And how did he know that *he* was the one I'd chosen to bring?

I rack my brain, wondering if I'd spoken it out loud in the hallway, but I don't believe I had. Rubbing the back of my neck, I gather my nerves and step inside, Agent Essex at my heels.

It is immediately warmer inside the apartment. I follow the direction the voice had come from, finding the owner sitting on a loveseat in a quaint living room. Afghans and multicolored throw blankets cover nearly every surface, except for the coffee table just in front of the couch.

Instinctively, I scan the room for threats. I don't find one, so I turn my attention to the man on the couch.

I expect, from the voice, to see a slender teenager, complete with round spectacles and messy hair—someone who belongs in a library, combing through ancient tombs and past wonders, maybe.

Instead, the Black man on the couch is even larger than I am, though unlike me, he's kept his hair natural, allowing it to grow into a full, tousled Afro around his face. He still looks young, though I can't pinpoint his age. He *feels* older. There's a calmness surrounding him that only comes with age.

When he smiles, his teeth are a blinding white.

"I'm Commander Aries. One of my agents said you asked for me?" I say, and while I don't mean it to be a question, it definitely comes out as one.

"The spirits have a message for you," the man answers, gesturing toward the armchair on the other side of the coffee table directly across from him. Clearly, he expects me to sit. I hesitate, but it quickly becomes clear that he doesn't plan to speak until I do.

I perch inelegantly on the edge of the mauve seat, my knees a finger width from knocking into the table.

I don't intend to but my gaze sticks to the glass sphere resting at the center of the coffee table. A crystal ball but instead of a base, the man is using a crumpled Coke can. The heart is cloudy, shallow cracks spiderwebbing across the left side. As I stare, the fog inside seems to dance, twirling into abstract forms. Just as they start to take shape, I tear my gaze away, my heart pounding.

The last time I looked, what I saw…such horrible things…

I swallow down the memory and set my jaw.

"The *shew-stone* likes you," the man says, a smile on his lips.

I ignore his comment and tug out my little notepad and a pen. "Can you tell me your name, sir?"

He laughs. "Sir, he says. Did you hear that?" I look up from the paper but he's not staring at me or Essex. Instead, he's staring at the empty cushion beside him. "I know," he adds. "Never used to be polite, did he?"

"Sir?" I prompt, pen poised.

"You may call me Iseldir," he says, and I don't miss that he doesn't claim it to be his name.

"The brave soldier," I murmur as I write it down, the old stories flickering through my mind like memories.

"The fortune teller," he corrects, tipping his head toward the crystal ball again. "You've come for a prophecy."

"No?" Again, it comes out, unintended, as a question. "We're hunting a Whisper. My men said—"

"Your men said I asked for you, which I did. You may think you are hunting a Whisper, but they are just a pawn in a larger game," Iseldir corrects me with the gentleness of a parent to his child and I bristle at the tone. He continues as if he doesn't notice, though his eyes are sharp. "You are out of time, Aries, Prince of Faerie."

He makes a choked sigh. The dark orbs of his eyes go milky white, and a chill settles on the air. When he speaks, his voice echoes, as if it is coming from a great distance. Immediately, I recognize a prophecy—a *true* fortunetelling—when I hear one, and I struggle to write it, word for word, on my note pad.

When you have nowhere left to fly,
And your breath seems
Endless bated,
And there's no one left to care,
That his bloodlust is unsated.

When scarlet turns the sky,
And that which cannot fall
Has faded,
Then Death will ride her Nightmare
To the City of the Dead.

Find the answers that you're seeking
In the sallow light of moonbeams

In the shadow of the valley
When you fear you've lost it all.

When his memories start seeping
Bringing poison to his daydreams
To stop Death's grand finale
By blade, the Lover falls.

The milky white drains from his eyes and his shoulders sag. I stare down at the notepad, reading the words again. The City of the Dead…? Could it mean Orleans? I haven't spent much time there, since they have their own dedicated branch of the BAA already.

I *don't* miss the reference to "*his bloodlust,*" and anxiety coils in my belly like a snake. We did the right thing by locking Leviathan up, so *surely* it doesn't mean him, right?

"Well, that doesn't sound *great,*" Agent Essex mutters.

"Always an optimist," I reply absently, inwardly agreeing. This was a doomsayer prophecy if I ever heard one—not my favorite kind, to be sure. Lifting my hand to my comm, I say to Agent White, "Call headquarters and tell them to have the Orleans' office keep an eye out for anything strange. Portents, ravens, you know the drill."

"Sir? It's Orleans…" Agent White says.

Good point. "Fine. Tell them to look out for anything strange for *Orleans.*"

Agent White goes quiet for several seconds, and his voice is hesitant when he finally says, "Boss? What's strange in Orleans?"

Another good point. "Just…tell them to keep an eye on the sky."

"Will do, Commander," Agent White replies.

After reading the prophecy one last time, I flip the notepad closed and shove it into my pocket. "Well, thank you for the prophecy, Iseldir. If you think of anything else, please don't hesitate to call." I snag a business card from my wallet and drop it on the coffee table by the crystal ball.

Iseldir gives a small, sad smile. "I don't think we will be meeting again, Commander Aries."

* * * *

Daddy

I can't hold them much longer.

I've lost count of the number of links joining me to the others. My essence feels flat and stretched, like the edges have been caught by a hundred tugging, yanking hooks. Power, leeching from the souls of the other prisoners, pumps down each link, and I can feel it pulsing in tune to my heartbeat.

I'm stuffed with it, on the brink of overflowing. If it were food, my belly would be round and bulging. I'm nearly out of time, but I don't know if it's enough. Could I grab another link or two? Build up that little bit more power? Would it be the difference between success and an implosion?

I don't know, and I can't risk it. Even one more link might be too much. I close my eyes and offer up a prayer — not to the Ether my people worship but to the Horned God of the fae. *Let Aries survive this.*

I can't stall my plan until I know for sure he's out of the city, even if I *had* a way to convince him to leave — which I don't, anyway. All I can do is hope his God keeps him safe from the harm I'm about to bring to this city and all who dwell within it.

Hope, because I won't change my plans. Eryn is everything to me. Without him, what use is this world of pain and suffering?

Besides, even if I *wanted* to back out, I can't. It's too late. I've gathered too much power, gorged myself on it to bursting, and it needs to go *somewhere*. If I don't let it out, then it will go *in*.

I'd seen it happen only once, and it looked like a terrible way to die.

I cannot die now, when Eryn needs me. Letting out a breath, I push myself to standing and focus my attention on the locked door. No matter how well they've reinforced it, it's still always going to be the weakest point in the room.

Then, I look into myself and find the hundreds of red strands, thick and pulsing, and follow them down, deeper into my essence, until I reach the well of my power. It's stretched, swollen—like an overfull bladder, just this side of causing pain. With a single, sharp motion, I puncture it.

Power erupts from my body. I do my best while I'm still conscious to aim it toward the door, and for the most part, it works, though enough escapes that in seconds, I'm standing in a swirling vortex of energy.

The door breaks as the world turns red.

Chapter Twelve

Pet

As soon as the door opens, the hinges silent on the night air, Moonlight strikes us. Nine, who had started to run as soon as it was clear, groans, stumbling to his hands and knees—paws and knees, I realize—just feet from the tree line. The other omega, the unshifted one, doesn't even make it that far before he falls to the call of the Goddess. Eight, already shifted, darts off without us.

The sound of their bones realigning is too loud, and I cringe, waiting for the alphas to hear us and come running.

There is only the song of the whip-poor-wills in the trees.

The remaining two wolves stand quickly, shaking out their fur. Nine is the smallest, though still he'd be bigger than mine if I were shifted beside him, his fur a tawny brown, except for the glints of red. Five is darker, a solid color somewhere between black and brown.

They dart into the woods, following the other omega, the one who had shifted in his cell. My heart breaks as I watch them leave. I hope wherever they end up, they are safe.

Three is still in my arms.

I stagger across the empty space and finally, *finally* he starts to shudder. I lay him down at the base of the first tree, watching his bones realign below his skin. His shift is painfully slow but eventually, a reddish-orange wolf has taken his place. He reminds me of a fox, ears slightly too large for his small frame.

My own refuses to come.

I glance up at the Goddess Moon. "*Please, Mother,*" I plead with her. On two legs, I will never be fast enough to be free.

A scarlet haze shimmers in the sky, and Moon goes red. My heart skips.

Is this my answer? Blood in the sky, foreshadowing my future. But then I feel it—my wolf, stirring in my chest—and I whimper in relief.

And suddenly, we're not alone anymore. A tawny wolf—Six, I realize, though not before I flinch away—nudges my arm, his own whimpers loud in the night air. I don't know what changed his mind, what made him come back, but I'm grateful he did. Something about his presence helps trigger my shift.

My wolf is achingly slow to come, breaking my bones almost one at a time, but after what feels like ages, he and I are standing on four paws, shaking out our fur. Nine gives a happy yip before he starts to run.

My wolf and I bump our shoulder into Three, gesturing with our muzzle toward the north. He moves slowly, as if he's testing the ground with each paw, and I wonder how long it's been since he's been outside.

I nudge him again, urging him to go faster, and with a little whine, he does.

The other omegas are out of sight, their scent heading west. Clearly, they've decided to go their own way, but after what they've gone through, I can't blame them. How long had they been there? Long enough, I was sure, that the thought of trusting another pack was too much to bear.

I wish them well, yearning to follow them, to convince them to join us, but my wolf rumbles a growl.

North, he demands, and I don't fight him on it. I've never heard him so clearly before.

I've never been this…*present* before, on a full moon or elsewise. I've always felt like my wolf came out and I went away—disappeared into a void, then woke up somewhere new. As a child, it had been terrifying.

Maybe that was why I used to struggle so hard with my shifts, always fighting to not be shoved aside or pushed down. I'd been afraid of disappearing…my wolf coming out and me just…going away, forever.

My wolf's warm presence nudges me, but it isn't angry or violent. It's almost…like he is trying to comfort me.

Together, he promises, and it is only one word, but it holds a wealth of meaning that somehow, I understand.

From now on, we are in this together. He isn't going to push me down anymore as long as I promise not to do the same to him.

We could be two separate beings living together in harmony.

I'd asked my old alpha once, when I was still a pup, what his wolf felt like to him. And I'd seen his answer on his face—the confusion, then the slow realization as his eyes widened. "Our wolves are us, Eryn. Just…us."

And there'd been pity, and it had been too much for me to handle, so I'd run away into the woods to my little patch of lilies, my heart pounding at the realization that I was broken.

Not broken, my wolf says now. *Just different.*

And maybe he's right. So what if my wolf isn't just me in a different body. So what if other werewolves don't have these silent conversations like I do. Does it matter, if we are happy?

What's your name? I ask him, allowing myself, for the first time, to acknowledge him as an equal.

Happiness fills me, and I know that it isn't mine, but his.

Lily, he answers.

Surprise fills me, but he keeps running, paws hitting the dirt fast. He's nimble, and I can tell he wants to go faster, but we don't, so Nine and Three can keep up.

Are you...a girl? I ask, tentatively. I don't want to break our newfound alliance by insulting him...her?

The wolf laughs, amusement flowing to me easily. *I am just wolf.*

Well, Lily, I reply, *it's really nice to meet you.*

They don't answer, but I feel their happiness.

By the time the sun rises, light filtering through the leaves above us, we've crossed two dozen roads, some busier than others, even late at night, and the three of us are flagging. Three, particularly, seems to be struggling, limping along with his head hung low.

Lily leads us to a small clearing with a bed of moss instead of grass, then I feel them curl up in my chest and suddenly, I'm shifting. It goes faster this time, smoother, and the pain is hardly anything, at least compared to what I'm used to. In moments, I am kneeling, naked, on the ground, my fingers curling into the soft green moss.

Nine and Three collapse beside me. Three doesn't shift, but Nine does, not seeming to care about his nudity or the dirt below him as he sprawls out in a patch of grass with a sigh.

"I haven't heard or smelled anyone following us," Nine says suddenly, breaking the quiet. "Have you?"

I shake my head. "No, I haven't." And while I'm grateful for that, I have to wonder why not. Hopefully, the alphas are just now getting back to the packhouse and will be too tired from their runs to visit the mollyhouse until at least noon. Could we get that lucky?

"Do you think they followed the others instead?" Nine asks, his voice small. He might have pretended, back there at the mollyhouse, to be an uncaring asshole, but clearly he feels more than he lets on.

"I don't know," is the only answer I can give. My gaze drifts to Three. He was the favorite, at least until I fucked everything up for him. Well, except for One and Two, the only omegas permitted to live in the packhouse itself, the personal property of Alpha Dixon's second and third in command.

Wouldn't the pack have followed Three's scent?

Nine follows my gaze and winces. Three is curled up nose to tail, his breathing slow with sleep. "They'd have followed us," he mutters eventually, like he's talking to himself. There's a resolve to his voice, almost like he's preparing himself for the worst.

He turns back to me and says, his voice a bit louder, though not so loud that it will carry beyond the clearing, "He's the old Alpha's son. Alpha Brant was a good man. He worked in the mines right alongside his men, and his omega did her turns with the laundry. Three was only five when Dixon challenged his father and took over the pack. I came later, of course, but I've heard the stories. Dixon killed his whole family and was going to kill him, too, but something stopped him. No one knows what, but he lived with Dixon until he hit puberty, then something changed." Nine's fingers pluck at the moss as he fidgets.

"What happened?" I ask, curious. I know I shouldn't, that if Three wanted me to know his past, he would tell me himself, but I can't help it. I tell myself that it's strategic—the more I know about him and Nine, the more I can anticipate Dixon and his pack's reaction—but I know I'm lying to myself.

"If anyone knows for certain, they weren't saying," Nine says with a shrug. "But there was a rumor that Dixon tried to take him as a mate instead of a ward, and he fought back. This was his punishment."

I cringe. What would I have done if that were me? If Alpha Carrick had come to me and said, "Mate me or else?" Would I have had the strength to say no? And to *keep* saying no, every time he asked after, knowing that doing so would keep me in that place?

Because now, the question Dixon had asked every time I heard him enter Three's room made sense.

"Have you changed your mind?"

And every time, Three had replied, *"I won't."*

And Dixon's voice had always been so cold when he replied, as if he were reading from a script, *"Then so be it."*

Then I'd had to listen to Dixon fucking the boy, and Three's stoic silence throughout.

I rub my palm over my chest as I stare at the small, sleeping wolf. I don't think I could have done it in his place. I'd have allowed the mate bond eventually. Maybe I'd have held out a month or two but years?

I don't think I'm that strong.

"We should get some sleep," I say, as I lie down on the moss. I don't want to think about it anymore, so I close my eyes to end the conversation. Nine is quiet, but then there is a sigh, and I hear him shifting.

I'm exhausted, but sleep takes a long time to come.

Chapter Thirteen

Aries

"Commander!" Agent White shrieks in my ear, my comm going staticky. I look to Agent Essex in concern then the two of us are sprinting out of the apartment. I skid to a stop.

Agent White is standing by the window at the end of the hall, one hand planted on the glass. He looks over his shoulder at us, fear plain on his face, and I start moving again.

Joining him, I peer out at the street, looking for whatever alerted him. It doesn't take long to see what it is, even in the dark. Dozens of people are sprinting down the street, and though I can't hear them from up here, I can see the way their mouths are open as they scream. In the midst of the frenzy, a half-demon — not a fullblood, thank gods, he lacks the horns — bellows, his eyes glowing red with rage.

"What the…?" I say, then choke off my curse as the three of us barrel for the stairs instead. We spill onto the sidewalk and almost immediately get knocked about by the fleeing crowd.

I look in the direction they are running from and freeze.

A Blood Storm rages on the horizon. The writhing, scarlet clouds crest higher than the skyscrapers in the east—right over where the Bureau of Arcane Activity containment cells are.

When scarlet turns the sky…

A lump forms in my throat, and horror corrodes my belly.

I fumble for my comms. "Aries to Base, what the hell is happening?" I fear I already know—there's only one Bloodwraith in the country, and I locked him in those cells myself. That Blood Storm is going to drag every person in the city with even a drop of demon blood into a frenzy.

The City of the Dead was never Orleans…

If Levi just escaped, then…

Static fills my earpiece, mingled with the sound of screams in the background, until a young voice cuts over it. "S-sir? Sir, he got out. There's blood everywhere, and I c-can't… Oh God, he killed Director Graves, just ri-ripped her throat out." The voice is unfamiliar, which means he must be one of the new hires, straight out of training.

My gaze meets Agent White's. The man is as pale as his name, nearly glowing in the night. I look to Agent Essex. His hands are shaking.

I draw in a breath and try to stay calm. Someone has to. I mute my comm and turn to the two agents I have with me. To them, I say, "Don't go back to headquarters. I want you to get to the nearest police station and grab as many officers as you can. Have them reach out to the other precincts and set up a temporary base *outside* the city limits."

"But what about the people…?" Agent White waves toward the fleeing Blanks, the ones we will be abandoning if we go through with it. Even as we watch, friend turns against neighbor, snapping teeth and raking claws, drawing blood with ease. I flinch as an old woman grabs what I think is her granddaughter and starts to bite her, her dull dentures shredding through the screeching child's skin. There's no saving her…no saving any of them.

"It's too late. If they get out, that's great, but we can't evacuate everyone. There's no time." I say, feeling heartless, even as I know it's the only way. "You have your orders," I snap, my voice harsh when they just stand and stare. They take off at a sprint to the BAA sedan on the street, the one Agent Mick and his team had left for them.

As soon as they are clear, I turn my comm back on.

"Officer—"

"She didn't even scream, and he just dr-dropped her like *trash*. There's so much blood. It's—" His fear comes through clear over the feed, tugging at something long buried in my chest.

I can't afford to unearth it now. I shove it back down with a ruthless growl as I snap, "Officer! Breathe, and tell me where you are."

I run for my bike and leap off the curb to straddle it, grateful for the custom leather seats that keep me from coming in contact with the Old-World Steel. It powers on with a push of a button, the rumble loud and angry.

"I…" He sucks in a ragged breath I can hear even through the staticky comms. "I'm in a service elevator. I think it's stuck."

"Does he know you're there?" I ask as I peel out onto the street, driving toward the churning scarlet storm. I hate to consider how many of my fellow agents have already perished to fuel it, how many agents my best friend had murdered in his rage.

"No, I…I don't *think* so," the young agent says, dropping suddenly into a whisper.

I should have stayed. What use was a prophecy given moments before the event? Maybe, if I'd been there when the tourmaline binding spell had worn off, I could have reasoned with Leviathan. It isn't like I don't understand his pain. A newly formed bloodbond is a sensitive thing, even when it forms out of a platonic relationship — which Leviathan and his little wolf certainly don't have.

Having his bound partner stolen from him? Well, that would make any demon crazy. One as powerful as Prince Leviathan, though…? The thought makes me twist the throttle that last little bit farther.

I'm no match for Levi, but I need to try, not just for the young agent on the other end of the comm but for the city. If I can't talk Levi down, he'll destroy it all — and likely his little wolf with it.

All around me, the Blanks that aren't trying to flee on foot scurry off the sidewalks toward their apartments, like the cheap drywall will protect them from the wrath boiling over on the horizon. I take a corner at a sharp turn, fast enough that I nearly overbalance. A woman screams, gathering a wailing toddler in her arms as she scurries up the steps of a hotel, nearly tripping over a teenage boy nursing a cigarette.

"Sir? Are you still there?" The young agent's voice shakes as he whispers in the earpiece.

"I'm on my way. Hold tight and stay put. If he doesn't know you're there, it's best to keep it that way," I say, angling around a horse-drawn buggy blocking most of the lane. The driver flips me off. A flash of my police lights has him dropping his hand like it caught fire, but I don't slow.

"I'm scared," the boy—*Officer*, I correct myself— whispers. I want to reassure him, tell him everything will be fine, but I'm fae, and I cannot lie.

"Keep quiet," is the best I can offer.

Headquarters looms out of the industrial thicket, wrought-iron fencing bent like brambles around the drive. Leviathan is still in there. I can hear the screams, *feel* the overpowering aura like static on my skin. I abandon my bike by the curb to pick my way through the mangled gates, cringing at the burn of iron.

I knew, when the higher-ups installed it, that someday it was going to piss me off. Crawling through its corpse costs me precious seconds. By the time I reach the front door, the unstormable building is quiet.

Too quiet.

I know the young officer is alive, his ragged breathing is still in my ear, but I don't hear any movement—no gunshots or yelling, no harried orders or commands. The only sound is the creaking of the door as I push it open.

The white walls are painted red.

Scarlet sprays cover the glass and make fingerprint-shaped trails along the linoleum, leading toward the stairway going up. My heart sinks. Leviathan is heading for the roof.

I unholster my weapon, regret filling me. I'd swapped the bullets out after I left the containment cells, some instinctive foresight urging me to be prepared. I'd never told Leviathan I'd ordered these. They were my "worst case scenario" backup plan, my "just in case" over-preparedness.

The tourmaline bullets are the only weapon I have that could stop him.

I can only hope they won't kill him.

The thought strikes me in its hypocrisy, that I would be worried for his life after the slaughter he's left behind him, but he is still my friend. My *brother*, if such a thing were possible.

I take the stairs to the roof.

Leviathan is dressed in blood where he stands on the building's edge, holding a corpse to his lips. What used to be an agent is now a broken doll, his arms hanging like a cord-cut puppet. The body's eyes are still open, unseeing but fixed with horror. Levi's are closed tight, furled beneath his heavy brows.

I draw in a breath and lift the gun.

Shoot, my instincts warn me. *Now, while he is feeding, while he is distracted, before he sees you or, worse, takes to the sky.*

I can't do it.

"Levi," I call, stepping closer. My hand shakes, but I refuse to lower it. "Let him go. We can talk about this. You don't need to do this."

Leviathan growls as he drops the body. It bounces on the cement, the skull shattering with a noise that will haunt my dreams. He turns fiery eyes to me and in them, I see no recognition.

He is a rabid beast.

He snarls something in a language I recognize but can't understand and stalks closer, blood dripping from his fingertips and staining his steps.

"Levi," I warn, backing away, "don't make me shoot you."

Leviathan's smile twists, then he opens his jaw. I know it's not real, that it's a side-effect of the aura he sheds like a caul, but his mouth gapes wider, a thousand dagger-teeth gnashing in threat.

His voice crawls out from between them like spiders. "Soon, your corpse will dance under our flesh and fuel us."

"Think of Eryn," I plead, hoping the boy's name will jar him from his rampage. "Your boy needs *you*, not your monster. Don't you want to bring him home?"

"He is *mine*." Levi's eyes go black, and a small sliver of hope flickers in my chest. At least he said 'mine', not 'ours.' Some remnant of Levi must remain, buried under the Legion.

"Come back to us, Levi," I say a bit louder, halting my retreat. I don't lower the gun, but I struggle through the oppressive aura to meet his eyes. "You can't save him like this."

Levi hesitates. I see the indecision, the flicker of uncertainty. His scarlet eyes dim, and I almost relax.

Then, a gunshot rings through the silence. Levi stumbles, red spraying from a hole in the neck. It gapes, the edges pulsing grotesquely, before it stitches itself closed like it was never there. "Wait," I holler to the young officer I only now spot creeping up the stairs, his face white but hands steady as he points the weapon at Levi.

He doesn't. Two more bullets tear into Levi's chest, sending him stumbling back a single step before they close. Fire flares in his eyes again, and I dive to the side, ducking behind the jutting protrusion of an aluminum ventilation shaft with a curse.

"Shit, shit, shit," the young officer is crying. Peeking around the corner, I see him fumbling with the chamber of his gun, bullets flying out as he tries to reload it. Leviathan stalks closer, a nasty smile twisting his lips.

His voice seems to echo as he speaks, like a thousand beings are talking in harmony. "Your bullets cannot harm us, little flesh boy. We will rend your skin from bone and drain you."

I raise my gun, but even before I can fire, Leviathan has snatched the officer up, slaughtering him like a pig. He rips his entrails through his mouth and is tying them around the officer's neck like a noose when I fire my weapon.

The bullet strikes him in the shoulder.

Leviathan screams, but the bullet doesn't lodge in bone and bind him. I see it strike the brick on Levi's other side, a through-and-through shot that seems to do nothing but piss him off. I curse and fire again, but now Levi is expecting it. He dodges, then he is in front of me.

His eyes are blank as he stares into mine. They are the last thing I see before he strikes like a cobra, his fangs piercing my neck and sending me tumbling into the blackness.

Chapter Fourteen

Eryn

I wake to thunder.

Shaking the other two awake, I say, "It's going to rain. We should get moving." Hopefully, the rain will wash away our tracks and dampen our scents, but I'm worried that it will slow the other two down, as well.

Three, still a wolf, stands and stretches, his mouth gaping in a wide yawn before he shakes, his ears floppy. Then, he sits, wagging his tail slightly. Nine just groans and throws an arm over his eyes. "Fuck, I forgot how much I hated being outside." Slowly, he uncovers his face and glares at the trees surrounding us. "It's kind of creepy. How much farther do you think we have?"

I look around. One tree looks much like another, and a deep breath in brings only unfamiliar scents, so I shrug. "A day, maybe?"

Yes, my wolf confirms. *Faster on four feet.*

Yes, I agree, then I...wait. I don't know how to start the shift, not on my own. The wolf sends their amusement to me then I feel them swelling inside me, guiding the change so I don't have to. Soon, the three of us are wolves again, and we run.

It starts to rain. The first drop hits Lily's nose and the wolf cringes back, sneezing. It takes me a second to notice the way the water smells—sour, like rotten eggs.

Beside us, Nine yelps, sidestepping to hide beneath the boughs of an evergreen tree, his ears tucked back. Even Three whimpers, slowing to a stop and huddling down. Then my wolf shoves me, forcing the shift, and I land on my hands and knees in the mud.

Lily huddles inside my chest, and I can feel their disgust.

As a human, at least, I can hardly smell the stench. I turn to the other two and wave them out. "Shift. It's not so bad."

Nine shifts first. He coughs as soon as he's human, then grimaces at his bare feet sinking into the squishy mud. "Smells better, but still feels gross." After a second, though, his lips quirk up in the tiniest smile. "Better than being back there, though."

Nine turns to Three and crouches down, running his fingers through the smaller wolf's scruff. "Come on, Three. It really is better like this."

Three twitches his ear, but he makes no move to shift. Instead, he straightens up and sticks his nose in the air. He wrinkles it then gives a cute little sneeze before he steps out into the rain. It flattens his fur quickly, and he's clearly miserable. I can't force him to change, and even if I could, I wouldn't.

He deserves the chance to make his own decisions.

Walking through the slippery mud on two legs is so much more difficult than on four. I fall more often than I feel like counting, and by the time the strangely red sun is at its peak, I'm more mud than flesh. Nine looks even worse than I do. His chestnut red hair is matted with dirt and sticks, his skin so coated that he hardly looks naked.

It draws a snicker from my mouth when I notice, and Nine glares at me. "What?" he snaps, picking himself up from the ground again. "You've fallen just as much as I have!"

"No, sorry... I was just thinking we look like we're wearing mud suits," I explain, gesturing down at myself.

Nine looks me over, then himself, then snorts as well. Even Three chuffs out a sound reminiscent of a laugh. "Don't worry," I say, standing still for a second and holding out my arms, letting the rain, which is finally starting to dwindle, wash away at least the top layer. Brown streaks down my skin and to the ground. "My pack will have baths you can use," I say as we start to walk again.

They can use. Not me, though, since I doubt they'll let me step more than two feet onto the territory before they drag me before the pack elders for a tribunal. I try not to let my fear show.

Nine and Three, at least, will be safe.

I lift my hand to the collar around my throat, the one that isn't Daddy's but reminds me of it. *Daddy will be devastated.* I wonder if I can get the omegas to the territory edges then leave before anyone in the pack spots me.

But if I leave, I'll have to tell Nine and Three *why*. I don't want them to know the kind of person I am — the kind who would kill his Alpha, the man who practically raised me, in cold blood.

Didn't do it, Lily chirps up, anger in their voice.

I stumble, barely catching myself with a hand against the closest tree. *What do you mean? Beta said...*

Lied. We killed turkeys, Lily says. Slowly, an image forms behind my eyes, like I'm watching a movie on an old film reel, faded and two dimensional. Me, as a wolf, chasing big birds through a soft dusting of white powder. *Snow,* I think absently. Us tearing the birds apart, then rolling around in a bed of flowers.

No Alpha in sight.

Anger burns me. Beta...lied? But why? What did he get out of telling me that I killed Alpha, and that the pack wanted me dead in return?

Me gone, I realize. I wish I knew why he hates me so much, but I suppose his reasoning doesn't matter. Lots of wolves hated ferals, and I'd grown up hearing the whispers of what happened to *other* ferals in *other* packs. I'd always considered myself lucky to live with the Havenwood Pack, instead. They might have ignored me, but they didn't try to *kill* me.

Beta must have hated ferals even more than I realized.

I rub a hand over my chest to soothe the hurt. That meant he didn't take me to the Flesh Market to *save* me. He probably *hoped* they would kill me, that way his hands could stay clean but he could still get rid of me.

"That *bastard*," I snarl out loud, the words echoing in the otherwise silent woods. Beside me, Nine flinches, lifting a hand like the sound startled him. "Sorry," I apologize immediately. "I just...I was thinking out loud."

"Wanna talk about it?" Nine says after a second, hesitation in his voice.

"I don't know," I answer honestly, then I sigh. "I'm so *stupid*."

"You were smart enough to get us out of there," Nine answers, his voice sharp. He lays a hand on my biceps and squeezes. "Whatever you think happened, I guarantee it wasn't because you were *stupid*."

"I trusted someone I shouldn't have," I say, my voice soft.

"So did I. So I must be a real fucking idiot."

I look at him in shock, my mouth opened to protest, but then I hesitate. "No. No, it wasn't your fault," I finally say, then I give him a small smile. "And I suppose it wasn't mine, either."

"Now *that's* what I want to hear," Nine says, and his smile is bigger now, showing his teeth. "*Next* time, we'll bite first, and ask questions later. Am I right?"

I laugh. "Yeah. Yeah, I guess we will."

Then a familiar scent tickles my nose and I pause, head turning toward it.

"What?" Nine asks, sounding afraid as he puts his nose in the air as well. Three tucks himself against my side, his tail clamped tight to his body.

"We made it," I breathe out, relief flooding me.

Maybe, if Beta lied…maybe Alpha is still there. And *maybe*, he won't kill me on sight.

Chapter Fifteen

Raving Rory/Ruairi

The city is burning.

Screams and smoke and people racing around like ants, and none of it concerns me. The city is always on fire, people are always screaming, and I am, now and always, on the sidelines — waiting, watching.

But the shadowy figure stumbling into the alley — *my* alley — that's another matter entirely.

He concerns me.

The Black man is bleeding.

I stand safe in my shadows, watching him stagger along the alley. One hand drags along the dirty bricks like the wall, seemingly the only thing keeping him upright. Considering the shape he's in, it might be.

I've seen him before.

I know this the same way I know that the grass in Omaha is green, even though I've never been there. The memories are there, but I can't *feel* them. They've been hidden away behind magical plexiglass. I can watch them like a movie. Hear them, even. But the emotions are…missing.

Nowadays, the man goes by some silly name. Apollo, or…Aries, that's it. A name not fit for a fae prince who passed his infancy long before the Greek myths were even born. When I knew him, he went by Aodhan. Of course, he'd never trusted me with his *true* name.

I'd trusted him with everything.

My body…my heart.

He'd broken both.

Now, he's the broken one. I see the blood staining his neck and hands blue, so different from the scarlet they'd painted me. Why is he here? This is *my* valley. *Mine*. I mapped each crack in the mortar, pressed fingertips against each brick.

The mural that Aries stumbles into was conceived in *my* dreams and painted by *my* hand, with pigments I ground myself and mixed with *my* own blood, with runes to bind the memory.

Aries—such a stupid name—breaks the Binding with one careless brush of his blue-tinged hand. The memory slams into me with the force of a freight train, and my knees buckle.

The smell of honeysuckle.

Grass silk-soft under my soles.

Windchime laughter on the autumn breeze.

I shake away the painful memory. Seeing his face is hard enough without the memory of his lips brushing mine fluttering around in my head. Hesitation dogs my steps, keeping me in the shadows until Aries stumbles again.

He catches the wall and starts to sink down. After everything, I should back away—retreat through the tunnel I'd painstakingly dug behind the dumpster for easy access into the basement squat I call home.

Instead, I step into the moonlight and stare down at his unconscious body. If he opens his eyes, he won't recognize me—not now, not like this. This body is older, if not wiser.

And not stronger, I notice as I try to lug his heavy, muscle-bound body over my shoulder. I fail quite epically and resort to dragging him instead. He takes a nasty fall as I shove his limp frame into the tunnel and lose my grip. His body bounces against the cracked cement below, and I cringe.

At least the Fae are resilient...

I slide down after him, landing softly in a crouch on my bare feet. Pressing my head to his chest proves his heart is still beating, if a bit slower than I'm used to. Wrapping my arms around his chest below his armpits, I start to drag him toward my corner. Despite the glamour I'd painstakingly cast, I know better than to keep anything valuable down here. I do, however, have a homemade first-aid kit tucked under my pillow.

I just have to get him there.

Old Joe curses me as I work. "Leave it to Raving Rory to drag in a fucking corpse. Like we ain't got enough messes down here, ya bedlamite. Last thing we need is maggots."

"Like they ain't crawling out of yer nasty teeth, you malodorous cockroach!" I snap back, but it comes out less savage than I intended as my breath catches in my lungs. "Shit, you've gotten *heavy*," I groan down at the unconscious man. In my memories, he is lanky and awkward.

This statue of a man is foreign.

I drop him on the pair of blankets I call a bed, wincing as his head smacks into the ground when I miss the pillow. "Oops." I almost feel guilty.

The first-aid kit is a bottle of vodka, a needle and half-a-spool of nylon thread, and a handful of Tylenol. Not much to work with.

At least the needle is silver, not iron.

Safe behind the veil of my glamour, I strip him down to the black briefs that do nothing to hide the girth of his soft dick, which I definitely don't stare at...*much*. I tear my gaze away and examine him for wounds. All I find is the large gaping one at the junction of his throat and shoulder. It looks like a bite wound, but not from any animal I've ever seen.

I have no idea where to start, how to gather the tattered edges back together.

Luckily, it takes more than a torn-open throat to kill a fae. If I had more than the accidental dregs of magic I stole with my botched spell, I could patch him up good as new. Instead, I bite my lip and hope for the best. My stitch job is raggedy, and the scars won't be pretty, but his glamour should cover them if he's still as vain as I remember.

People don't ever change—and fae are even more intractable than mortals. I can't hold in my snicker. He's going to be livid when he realizes the thread is hot pink.

If only I could be here to see it.

* * * *

Princeling

Drip.
Drip.

I flinch as something lands on my cheek, cold and wet like rain, but when I open my eyes, I don't see the sky. Instead, I'm staring at rotted wooden beams, spiderwebs clinging to the exposed nails.

This is *not* where I left myself.

I go to sit up, but something in my neck tugs almost painfully. When I reach up to find out why, I touch thread holding together healed skin. One, two, three…seventeen stitches in a jagged pattern from jaw to collarbone.

Whoever stitched me up did a decent job but hadn't factored in how fast I'd heal. The skin is gathered tight around the thread, bunched and — now that I notice it — mildly itchy.

It's going to be a bitch to cut them out later.

A hacking cough sounds from nearby, and I jerk up, realizing for the first time since waking that I'm not alone. On the other side of the unfinished basement — at least, that's what it looks like, I can't really be certain — a man with a scraggly beard is glaring at me. He has the protruding jaw of a man with no teeth.

Grimacing, I push myself up, chest heaving from the effort. *Would it be rude to plug my nose,* I wonder as I keep my eyes on the stranger, unwilling to look away. I know it's stereotyping — he could be a perfectly nice man, just because he's homeless doesn't mean he's a criminal — but something about him is off-putting. Not just the body odor, either.

There's a sharp edge hiding beneath his baggy, hole-ridden clothing. I don't need to see it to know that it's there. He has the look of a man who would cut a bitch from gullet to groin if it earned him a hill of beans.

"Where am I?" I grunt as I drop my hand back into my lap, feeling discreetly for my weapons. My heart drops into my belly. They're gone — both guns, even my knife. A subtle shake of my ankle proves that blade is missing as well.

Well, fuck.

"Crazy man, came in with the crazy man," he repeats, rocking side to side. *Who the hell brought me here if* this *lunatic thinks* they're *crazy?*

"Fuck!" I curse and jerk my hand up to my ear, feeling for a comm that isn't there. When I feel for my timepiece, it's missing. "What time is it?"

"You think I got a watch?" He shakes his bare, dirty wrist at me, then huffs. "Time for you to leave, anyway. Pointy eared motherfucker…" He says the last quieter, but not enough that I can't hear.

He's probably right, but when I try to stand, my head spins and I collapse back down onto my ass. The room is spinning. I press my palm to the side of my head, hoping to still it, but it doesn't help much.

Suddenly, a loud voice hollers from directly above me, the voice piercing yet achingly familiar. "What? My place not good enough for your royal head to rest, Princeling?"

"Ouch," I groan, squinting my eyes close as it triggers a migraine. "Not so loud."

"Drink too much faerie wine?"

"Ruari?" I ask, squinting as I try to see him, but it's as if the voice comes from nowhere. But it can't be him… I know it's impossible. *Is my mind playing tricks on me?*

Ruari ran away from me long before the Blanks discovered steam power. No mortal, no matter *how* well they took care of themself — and Ruari had never taken care of himself well — could have lived this long. Surely, the familiar voice is just that…familiar.

"I go by Rory now," he answers, a confirmation that makes no sense. Blanks don't live this long. He'd be…hundreds of years old, even if I *don't* consider the time he spent in Faerie. Since so few changelings ever survived returning to their world, it was hard to say what the effects of Faerie were on mortals.

He drops down from the shadows of the rafters, landing catlike on the cracked pavement a few feet in front of me.

"You look different," I say, out loud but quite by accident. Not *too* different though. I notice he's still wearing the necklace I gave him—a brass Celtic knot pendant, though it's hanging on a metal chain now instead of leather.

He's taller, but that's not the only difference. There's a coldness to him, a distance in his eyes that they'd never held before—and something else, a fading at his edges that I can only sense, not see.

"I changed. People do that, you know." He smiles. His eyeteeth are sharp and sallow.

"How...?" I let my voice trail off, not sure myself what I want to ask.

His laugh is hollow. "How did I find you? How did I change? Or how am I still alive?"

"Yes," I say, rather than ask the dozens of questions I *could* have asked.

"Fuck you, Aodhan-who-goes-by-Aries." Ruari— *Rory*, that's what he goes by, I remember—turns away, giving me his back as he stalks toward a small window high on the wall to the left. "You didn't care then. Why should you now?"

"I didn't care? *I* didn't care?" I repeat myself, stressing the word as incredulity swamps me. "You just...left. Disappeared in the twilight without a word, but you think *I* didn't care?"

He stills, looking over his shoulder with an expression cold as ice on his face, and it freezes the remainder of my protest in my throat.

I swallow around the lump of ice.

116

This is not the man of my memories.
This...this is someone else.

Chapter Sixteen

Pet

The packhouse is smaller than I remember.

Not literally... I know that it hasn't shrunk. It just *seems* smaller, compared to the luxury of Levi's mansion. Had I become that spoiled so quickly, just by a few weeks of freedom on his estate?

How had I never realized that the house's siding was so faded or that the porch tilted dangerously to the left? Or that the little garden behind the packhouse that the women worked so diligently on was hardly more than a patch of dirt, a few scraggly plants growing too close together in hopes of eking out that last little bit of food?

I rub my hand on my chest as the realization hits.

Maybe my pack had never hated me.

Were they quiet because they were exhausted from working themselves to the bone? Distant because I'd been another mouth to feed in a pack that already had too many?

I bite my lip before I pull back my shoulders, feigning courage—but I tangle my fingers in the scruff of Three's neck for strength. "There it is," I say as I scan the grounds for Alpha Carrick. I don't know who I can trust besides him. Were there others involved in Beta's plot? I have no way to know.

We're at the back of the packhouse, still hidden at the forest's edge. From here, I can see most of the property. Two women are kneeling in the garden. One is holding up the cold frame while the other peers under it, examining the root vegetables. Nearby, a man chops logs near the fire pit. It's not Alpha—his shoulders are too wide—so I keep looking.

"There," I say, pointing toward the side of the house. He's digging a shallow ditch near the foundation, under the sagging gutter. His back is bent, but even when Alpha straightens up, his back never does. *Did it always do that?* I wonder, watching Alpha Carrick lean the shovel against the side of the building and rub his hands.

"He's old," Nine says, and he seems surprised. "Has his pack not tried to challenge him?"

"Why would they? He's a good Alpha. His age makes him wise," I say, though it does make me wonder. Was there more to Beta's plot than just getting rid of me? Worried, I scan the yard again, but if Beta is around, he's not in sight.

There won't be a better time than this.

I step onto the lawn, the sunlight blinding after so long under the canopy of the forest. My eyes water, and I lift a hand to shield them, squinting toward the packhouse. Blinking away the shine, I start walking quickly forward, hoping to reach Alpha before anyone else notices me.

I make it halfway before I hear one of the women in the garden—Gloria, I realize, now that I'm closer—gasp. "Eryn? Is that him? Paisley, is that Eryn? Who's with him?"

I force my eyes away from the gossiping women and back toward Alpha.

He's staring at me, and his expression makes me freeze. There's no anger, just...shock. It fades quickly to a disbelieving sort of smile, then he's running toward me. I flinch, bracing for an impact that doesn't come. He stops just in front of me, his hand raised like he wants to touch me, but he doesn't.

Instead, he hovers it near my face, his voice shaking as he says, "Eryn? You've come home?"

Suddenly, the weight of the past few months—the fear, first of Levi, then of Puck and Dixon—slams into me, and I collapse forward with a sob. He catches me, gathering me against his strong chest. For the first time since that day in the hotel room when everything fell apart, I feel safe.

"I'm sorry," I cry between my choking breaths. "Please don't hate me."

Maybe I hadn't appreciated it before, maybe it took time and distance, but I realize now, cradled against him like a child, that he's the closest thing I've ever had to a caring parent.

When none of the pack couples had wanted me, it was he who'd taken me in, even though he was a single wolf with a pack to run, with duties and responsibilities that didn't include a broken pup who flinched at sudden movements and loud noises.

When I'd had nightmares, he'd told me stories until I fell asleep, dreaming of fairy tales and happily-ever-afters.

And when I'd told him that I wanted a new pack, one where I fit in, he'd never protested. Even though maybe, the thought of me leaving had hurt him more than I realized. He certainly seems happy now, to have me back.

"I could never hate you, child. I just wish you'd said goodbye," Alpha says, holding me a bit tighter, and when I finally look up at him, curious at the choked sound to his voice, I'm surprised to see him crying.

Alpha *never* cries. He hadn't even let himself after the summer he broke his ankle in a rabbit track, just days after the full moon. He'd spent almost a month limping around, stone-faced.

"I wanted to, but...I thought you were dead," I say, then bury my face in his chest when I add, "I thought I'd *killed* you." The words come out muffled, but not so much that he can't understand me.

He stiffens, arms tightening around me. He catches himself just before it becomes painful, breath catching audibly in his throat. After a second, he lets it out and nudges me back. "Explain." I open my mouth but then he cuts me off. "Wait. Let's get you inside and into some clothing. Your friends, too. I'm sure you're all starving."

"Oh, shit," I curse, jerking back and shooting an apologetic look toward the omegas. I'd almost forgotten about them standing behind me, overwhelmed as I was by seeing Alpha again. "This is Three and Nine. They escaped with me."

"Escaped?" Alpha practically yelped, then he swiped a hand over his face. "Boy, you got a story to tell, and I don't want to wait any longer to hear it."

He takes us inside and I'm surprised when he leads me upstairs—to my room, which is still there, almost exactly the way I left it. I swallow as I stare at my bed. It's been made and the sheets are clean, as if he wanted it to be ready for me, just in case I did come back.

He hadn't forgotten about me — hadn't been happy to finally be rid of the freak. He'd...he'd *missed* me.

Tears burn my eyes, and I try to discreetly rub them away.

Not discreetly enough, though, because Alpha shifts awkwardly beside me and says, "I always hoped you'd come home."

I step farther into the room and run my hand over the blanket. *The* blanket, the pink one Crazy Pat crocheted for me — the one that I told Three about while we were locked in that hellhole. And Three must recognize it, too. One second, he is a tail-tucked wolf at Nine's side, and the next, he's a naked young man, crouching at the side of the bed. He stretches out a hand to feel it, running the wonky stitches through his fingers before he looks at me with wide eyes.

"It's soft," he whispers. A second later, he seems to realize what he's done, because he makes a small *eep* and scuttles over to me, like he thinks he can hide behind my spindly legs.

Alpha Carrick is staring at Three with a slack-jawed, wide-eyed stare. I drop my hand to Three's head in a soothing gesture. After a second, Alpha Carrick blinks and clears his throat, lifting his gaze away from Three to meet mine. "Get dressed and come downstairs when you're ready. I'll...um. I'll get some food for you." He clears his throat again, looking uneasy as he hurries out of the room.

I stare after him for a second, then down at Three, who's staring after Alpha Carrick like he just saw a ghost.

Feeling like I missed something, I shake off the oddness and go to my dresser. Part of me expects it to be empty when I tug open the top drawer, but all my clothes are exactly where I left them, even the unmated socks shoved into the corner.

I throw an outfit onto the bed for myself but hand Nine and Three a set directly to them. "There's a shower through there," I say, gesturing toward the door next to my bed. "The water will be cold and there isn't a lot of water pressure, but it's private."

Nine turns to Three. His voice, when he speaks, is the gentlest I've ever heard it. "You go first."

Three looks at him and clearly hesitates, though I can't tell if he's surprised or grateful as he stands, still hunched over, and heads into the bathroom.

"That was nice of you," I say quietly, hoping my words don't carry over the sound of the water I just heard turn on.

"You were right to bring him with us. I never should have suggested leaving him." Nine turns his back to me and quite obviously changes the subject. "So this was your room?"

"Yeah," I answer, and I almost leave at that. Something inside me urges me to be honest, though, so I add, "I used to hate it. I thought…Well, I thought that Alpha only took me in because he *had* to, and that was why he gave me this room all the way up here, instead of having me bunk with the other unmated wolves in the dormitory downstairs."

Nine reaches out his hand and fiddles with the lamp on my nightstand. Alpha gave it to me when I was little and still having nightmares in the dark. It's a child's lamp, the shade a light blue, cloudy sky. "It's nice."

"Yeah," I agree. "I don't think I appreciated it the way I should have." And really, maybe I *had* been spoiled. What kind of person was given a private room, with furniture picked out specifically for them and got angry because they didn't have to share with the others?

Looking back now, a little bit older but with my rose-colored glasses off, I can't believe my naïveté. Of *course* Alpha wouldn't have put a pup in the dormitory with the young adults. Between the fighting, the posturing over territory and the fucking, it would never have been appropriate. It hadn't been a slight against me. It had just been Alpha being kind.

He could have shoved me in one of the linen closets, though, like the first couple I'd stayed with had. I'd been small enough, then. Or, he could have made me curl up in the kitchen near the fire, like the second family, one of the two breeding pairs in our pack. They'd had six pups of their own already and no room for a seventh.

Instead, he'd given me his room and started sleeping in his office, and why had I never noticed what that meant?

I sigh. "I was stupid."

"You were young. All of us are stupid when we're young," Nine said, shrugging.

In the bathroom, the water shuts off then a damp but dressed Three hovers in the doorway. "I'm done," he says, shifting his weight.

"You go next," I say to Nine, and he doesn't hesitate, moving past Three into the other room. He doesn't bother shutting the door behind him, clearly not concerned with the lack of privacy. After what he'd been through—what they'd all been through—I'm not surprised.

Three grips the hem of the oversized shirt, his fingers tucked underneath, out of sight. I'm not large, so the fact that he's swimming in my clothing is further proof of how tiny he is. "Do I have to go downstairs?" Three asks, his hesitance easy to see.

"You don't have to. I can bring you something to eat up here," I promise, then gesture toward the bed. "You can lie down, if you'd rather. I know I'm exhausted." Just thinking of it has me yawning, but it's not time for me to lie down yet. If I do, I'll never want to get back up, and I definitely need a shower before I touch anything else. The rain may have helped loosen some of the mud, but I feel like the rest has started to merge with my body.

Even a cold shower with cheap soap sounds great to me right now.

If Daddy were here, he'd make sure you were clean, a small voice says in the back of my head, and I ruthlessly shove it down. I can't think of that now—of Daddy's hands, warm and gentle, on my skin as he bathes me.

If I let the memories surface, they'll bring with them all the fear I've been trying to ignore—the worries that Daddy didn't survive the assault in the hotel room, that I'll never see his smile again or hear his laugh, that I'll never fear his hands on my skin, grounding me in the perfect moments we shared together...

Stop it! I scold myself and pinch my thigh, hoping the pain will distract me from the melancholy thoughts. And it does, a little—enough for me to make it through my icy cold shower when Nine finishes his, and enough for me to make it downstairs to share my story with Alpha Carrick.

Later, though, when the three of us are huddled together in my 'barely big enough for all of us bed', and the dark creeps into my bedroom, I find myself right back there, sinking into the achingly hollow memories.

And I find myself terrified that they are all I'll ever have of Levi—shadows of memories, doomed to be spoiled by the effects of time.

* * * *

Rory/Ruairi

"It doesn't matter," I say, my voice chilly, rather than question him further. Do I want to know what he means when he says I *'just left,'* as if I had a choice? As if he hadn't sent his personal guard to drag me from our bed just hours after I'd given him my body for the first—and only—time?

Of course I do, but I can't trust a single word out of his mouth. He might not be able to lie, but I know for a fact he can twist the truth until it might as well be a falsehood.

Once, he'd told me he loved me, and look where we'd ended up?

"You can stay until dawn. If you're here later, I won't be responsible for what happens." I leap, hooking my fingers around the windowsill and pulling myself up with ease. Now, in this body, it's easy to support myself with one hand while the other removes the latch.

"Wait! Rory, please..." Aries calls after me but I ignore him, squirming through the narrow space on my belly like a worm.

On your belly, worm.

The intrusive voice surfaces from the dark depths of the memories I'd tried to lock away, and I shove it away with a gasp. As soon as I'm safely in the alley, I push myself to my feet and start to run, aimless. I don't care where I end up, as long as it's not here.

I should never have lingered, watching him sleep in the sallow light of the squat I call home. I knew, even as I lifted myself to the rafters like a rat, that it was a bad idea. My memories of him were the only ones I'd never succeeded in abandoning, no matter how many runes I painted into murals, no matter how much blood I sacrificed to the pigment.

If Aries thought those memories were going to be enough to make me forgive him, he was wrong.

He'd have better luck convincing the ocean to burn.

Chapter Seventeen

Pet

I can't sleep.

I roll off the mattress and move silently toward my dresser. I grip the handle of the middle drawer and start to pull, remembering at the last second to lift up so it doesn't squeal. Once it's open enough for me to stick my hand in, I pull out my favorite sweater.

I don't remember where I got it from, just that I've had it since I hit puberty. It's my favorite because of its size. It falls to my knees and the sleeves fully cover my hands when I put my hands down, keeping them warm even in winter. There's no hood, which is its only downfall.

I tug it on, the neckline stretching over the iron collar, then I pull out a pair of handknit socks. Grateful for their thickness, I slip them over my chilly feet before tiptoeing back to the bed. Holding my breath—I don't want to wake either of the omegas now that they've finally fallen asleep—I crouch beside the bed and reach beneath it, pulling out a pair of worn sneakers. I don't put them on. Instead, I carry them with me to the door.

I've just cracked it open when I hear Nine say quietly, "Are you leaving us?"

I pause, hand on the door, and look back over my shoulder. "No, just going for a walk. Go back to sleep."

Nine narrows his eyes but eventually nods. "Be careful."

"I will," I promise. I'd like to say there's no reason to, but unfortunately, there is. Apparently, Alpha had sent Beta to a nearby pack to barter for supplies, and he was supposed to be back any day. If he sees me here...if he knows what I've told Alpha...there's no telling what he might do.

I know I shouldn't go outside.

I step into the hallway anyway.

I forgot how cold the packhouse gets at night, once the fire burns down to coals. Goosebumps erupt on my skin, and I rub my palms over the arms of my sweater to generate a bit of heat.

The chill doesn't stop me from stepping outside, though. The grass is crunchy from frost beneath the soles of my shoes, sounding loud in the silence of the yard, so I hurry toward the trees.

It's quieter beneath their shadows. I stop for a moment and breathe in the arctic air, nothing but evergreen and pine for miles. My nose twitches, catching a faint odor beneath it, one I almost missed. Something's died nearby...and recently. The scent isn't yet blighted with rot or decay.

My kind aren't the only hunters in these woods, though, so I just offer a silent prayer to Goddess Moon that I don't meet whichever wild beast just caught their dinner. With a fresh kill, I know they likely won't be hungry enough to attack, though they may get territorial.

Best to skirt around it, I decide, veering off the path to the east. I don't need the overgrown trail to find my way to my favorite lily patch anyway. I reach it just as the sun crests the horizon into the sky, golden light filtering through the bare limbs above me.

I settle into the largest patch of sunlight, the frost-coated grass chilly beneath me, and stare at the empty patch of dirt that will, come spring, birth lilies. I tuck my knees to my chest beneath the sweater, the fabric stretching, and cover my fingertips with the sleeves. Then, I drop my chin to my knees.

Could I learn to be happy here?

Maybe it's true what they say about trauma…that it numbs you. Now that I know Alpha Carrick is going to let me stay—let *us* stay, since he's extended an invitation for the two omegas to stay for as long as they choose—I should feel grateful. Right?

But staying here means accepting that I'll never see Levi again—that my Daddy is well and truly gone. Either dead, or unwilling to look for me, and I don't know which is worse.

I've done everything I can do from here. Alpha Carrick called the BAA headquarters last night and left a message with their switchboard operator, but he'd said afterward that the lady who took the message sounded harried, and she'd had no way of knowing when someone might be able to return a call.

I suppose I could ask Alpha to drive me back into the city, but with Puck still on the loose—and likely still searching for me, considering the stone resting heavy in my belly—it would be risky.

I'd hoped to safely pass the smooth rock by now. It could live out its days in the sewers, never traceable back to me. Unfortunately, I could still feel it. It is hard to ignore the pulsing heat it sends coursing through my stomach, especially out here in the cold.

If only Whisper hadn't made me swallow it, the old wix might leave me alone. It's not like I'm anything special, after all, except for Daddy's fascination with me.

Will this hollow aching in my chest ever fade?

Someday, maybe. That thought is almost *more* painful.

I told Alpha Carrick everything last night except for *this*. I'd told him that Levi had been kind to me, and that I was worried about him. I couldn't force out the rest — that I'm worried he is *dead*. Or worse, that he isn't, and he just no longer cares.

What will I forget first? I wonder as I stare, unseeing, at the patch of ground that used to bring me such comfort. *His voice, the way it grows softer when he speaks to me? Or the brush of his lips on mine? Or will it be the look in his eyes, that possessive claim he lays on my body?*

I don't want to forget anything.

Unless I could forget these last few days — *Has it only been a few days?*

A whine spills from my mouth. I slap a hand over it, smothering the sound, but it doesn't do anything to prevent the tears that burn my eyes until they leak out down my cheeks.

Has it been three days or four? *Not even a week and look at me. Weak. Nine and Three aren't out here sniveling like a pup, so why am I?*

Despite the chill, I start to sweat. I feel it beading on my forehead and the back of my neck. Hunching forward doesn't help. All I can feel is calloused hands dragging over my skin, pinching and poking and prodding, and Puck's face in my memory melts into Dixon's and back.

"Stop it," I shout…or try to. Instead, my voice comes out a shaky whisper. I lift my hands to my scalp, running my fingers roughly through my long hair, pulling by accident. But the pain helps, so I do it again.

As soon as I can breathe, I start talking to myself, hoping to bring myself down from the cliff my mind is dancing on. "You aren't there anymore. You're here, at Havenwood Pack. Alpha will keep you safe until Daddy comes. No one is going to hurt you now."

"I wouldn't be so sure of that."

* * * *

Princeling

The sky is barely starting to lighten as I struggle out of the squat. I can't help but notice it—the only way out of the rank-smelling basement is through the narrow window Rory had escaped out of. My shoulders are too broad to make it through, no matter how much I wiggle, and I'm stuck staring up at the smoke-filled sky.

Finally, I curse. For the first time in centuries, I adjust my glamour, and I hate it. I hate every second of it, and I know it's a petty concern, considering the shit that went down in this city last night. It says something about my entitlement—the selfishness I've struggled for years to outgrow—that a small part of me considered lying here, trapped, until the search and rescue teams came, just to avoid having to drop it, even for a second.

I hate the reminder that *this* is who I truly am—a thin-framed youth by fae standards, not the warrior I've forged myself into. As soon as I'm safely on the sidewalk, I pull my glamour back on, relaxing as I feel my shoulders reach their familiar breadth.

The last person I let see me like *that*, I realize, was Rory, all those centuries ago.

I don't have time to mull on that thought, though, because as soon as I leave the narrow alley, I stumble over a body. It's as bad as I expected, and yet expecting it does nothing to dull the horror.

I've fought in wars—*so* many wars, too many to count, too many for me to even name.

I've felt the warm blood of a fresh kill on my skin and held my enemy's beating heart in my hands.

I've cradled the thin, dying frames of nearly every lover I've taken in my arms as they died.

None of them had left me collapsed in the gutter like this, puking my guts out beside a body that was too small for me to think about.

Guilt tries to drown me. *This is my fault. If I hadn't hesitated on that roof... If I'd shot while I had the chance.*

Or, the more emotional side of me replied, *if you'd never arrested him in the first place. You knew he hadn't broken any laws.*

Yet, my practical side finished.

"Shut up," I scolded myself, heaving again. It doesn't matter whose fault this was. All that matters is fixing it.

But how do you fix this?

"First, find a phone," I mutter out loud, and start to search the bodies. "Just dead meat," I say out loud, and when I think of them like that, it becomes easier to rifle through their pockets, one after another.

Until I flip one and find myself face to face with someone I know.

The seer, Iseldir, his milky white eyes still open... His black skin is gray now and long cold. There's no hope of saving him. I remember his last words to me. *"I don't think we will be meeting again, Commander."*

Had he seen this? Known his own demise was creeping closer?

I force myself to leave his body and continue my search, but part of my mind lingers with him, wondering. It must have been such a burden...

Finally, I find a cell phone. It's an old model, still keyed to the owner's biometrics. I cringe a bit as I grab the man's thumb and press it to the screen, allowing the holo screen to flicker to life above the device.

The glowing blue keypad taunts me. I stare at the dial pad blankly. Who is even left to call, with headquarters destroyed and Director Graves dead? With shaking fingers, I input Agent Mick's number.

Three rings, then four. Five, and it switches to voicemail. I try again, a chill spreading through my chest when there's still no answer. I try Agent Essex next, with the same result. Finally, Agent White answers on my second try to him, his voice harried.

" —fuck! Get them off the street. I don't *care* if you don't have your orders from your supervisor. He's likely dead just like the rest. Get the street clear." It takes me a second to realize the man is talking to someone else, and wherever *they* are, the streets are a lot louder than here. All that surrounds me is silence and death. Then Agent White barks, "What?" and it takes me even longer to realize he's talking to me now.

"Look... I don't have *time* — " he starts to say.

I interrupt him. "It's Commander Aries. What's your location?"

"Commander?" His shock is easy to hear, even through the phone. "We thought you were a goner for sure! Someone spotted you going into headquarters right before it blew."

"Blew? It exploded?" *Fuck, how gone was I last night?* I remember the darkness in Levi's eyes right before he struck, the pain and the rest of the night was a blur until I woke up in the squat. Surely I'd have remembered an explosion?

"Well, not *literally.* Looked like one, though. Turned the whole sky red."

Agent White sounds like he's on the verge of going on a tangent so I stop him. "Agent, your location?"

"We've got a temporary base set up in Jersey. The Bureau's deployed agents from Chicago, Maine and Brunswick to assist. The first plane lands at noon."

That was a relief, at least. "How many of ours made it?" I ask, fearing the answer.

Agent White is quiet for long enough I hang my head in mourning. Couldn't be many, if it's taking him this long to answer. Our headquarters was home to almost two thousand agents, before the attack.

Finally, Agent White answers. "Fit for duty or overall?"

"Both," I say after a second's consideration. I want to know how many we lost, but knowing how many I can rely on to help restore — and keep — order is important as well. I start walking, scanning the streets for any working transportation. Even the horses have been slaughtered.

"Overall, we've located three hundred and seventy-nine of our agents. Of them, about half have been cleared for duty. We have an additional..." His voice gets muffled, like he's covered the microphone to confer with someone, then he comes back on the line. "Four hundred officers from various police precincts and around fifty members of the national guard. We've issued a call for assistance from any former or off-duty military personnel, as well."

"And civilians?" I ask, veering toward a side street when I see a bike tipped over against the sidewalk that doesn't look too damaged. Would I want to take it mountain biking with the handlebars like that? Probably not, but it will be faster than walking.

"I'd say we have about a million survivors, so far at least. Search and Rescue's only been in for an hour."

At first, it sounds like a lot—until I recall the latest census that had the population at nearly fifteen million. "Fuck," I curse, grief weighing at my chest. I take a moment to issue a prayer to whoever may be listening for the safe passage of their souls to their next lives.

"Around two thirds have been successfully relocated to stay with friends or family elsewhere. The Islamic Center has kindly opened their doors to house some of the remaining, and we've commandeered the local school buildings to place the rest until more permanent arrangements can be made."

I hesitate to ask the next question, but I need to know. "And...what about Levi?" *What am I hoping to hear? That he's safe? Or that he's been neutralized.*

"The Blood Demon? He hasn't been spotted since just after midnight."

"That many dead in so short a time?"

"Demon only killed a fraction. The rest was from either the hysteria or..." Agent White hesitates, then says, "Commander, when the demon escaped...he wasn't the only one."

Well, shit.

Leviathan...what have you done to us?

I drag in a breath. I close my eyes as I consider the plan slowly forming in my mind. *Levi will never forgive you,* a little voice whispers, and I shove it down. It's too far past that, now. For the first time since this whole mess started, I need to do what's best for the city, not my friend.

"Call the Harbinger." His title seems to resonate on the air, echoing at a timbre almost too low to hear.

I hear Agent White catch his breath, a soft, choked sound, then there is silence for a long moment before he says, "Are you sure?"

"I don't think we have a choice. Even if it was just..." My voice catches on his name but I swallow and say it anyway, "Leviathan... He's gone too far for us to walk it back now. Gods, the *bodies.*" My gaze locks on one as I pass, and I cringe, forcing it away. "And if the others are free as well?"

Agent White finally agrees. "As you say. I'll call for a Circle."

I catch movement ahead and my stomach drops. "Make it quick, Agent." Then, I end the call and shove the borrowed cell phone into my pocket. A kid—a teenager at most—stumbles farther into the street, falling to his hands and knees as a familiar female chases them.

"Xera!" I call, hoping to distract the lesser demon from her prey. She flinches, twisting at the waist to stare at me, her sharp, black teeth bared.

"Aries," she says with a snarl, completely forgetting about the young kid she'd been chasing. Trying to be subtle, I meet his gaze and tip my head toward an alley, and he scrambles to his feet to run toward it.

I know Xera must hear him — he's not quiet — but she has fixed her attention to me. I can't blame her. I was barely out of my rookie whites when my team took her down. The succubus had drained over a dozen men before we'd caught up to her. She took out half my team with a single flutter of her eyelashes.

Only my being gay had kept me safe from her compulsions.

I have no weapons, nothing to fight with but my magic, but I can't stand aside and let her feast on the survivors. She's lost weight since her imprisonment. Naked, it's easy to see the skeletal monster she's become. Each of her ribs is a washboard of bones.

We'd tried our hardest to keep the prisoners healthy, but it wasn't always easy. Rather, some of the prisoners hadn't *made* it easy. There was something wrong with Xera. A succubus, like their ankubhan brethren, should feed from the willing. We'd sent in volunteers weekly, but she'd snubbed her nose at each.

It was as if she'd adopted the traits of the incubus — a cousin of sorts, who preyed on the *unwilling*. They were one of the few species we put down on sight. There was no way to humanely imprison them without causing starvation, since no government in the world would justify rape to feed them.

"Turn yourself in, Xera. You know how this ended last time," I say, taking slow steps back, away from the alley and the kid escaping down it.

"Ha!" She laughs, then bares her teeth again. "Last time, you had an army and weapons. Now, you are alone and unarmed." She gives me a wicked smile. "I will enjoy feeding on you, Agent. But you...you will not enjoy it so much."

Chapter Eighteen

Daddy

I wake in a shallow pool of water, the stagnant stench sticking in my nose. With a groan, I roll over, splaying my arms out against the hard cement of what feels like a sidewalk. When I finally force my eyes open — something is sticking, clumpy, to the lashes, holding them together like glue — I grimace at the sight that meets me.

The puddle I'm lying in isn't street water. Rather, it is clotted, reddish-brown blood, just old enough to start turning rancid. I hate the smell of dead blood. It's harsh and acrid and even in the smallest quantity, it makes me want to sneeze.

And this?

This was *definitely* a bloodbath.

I try to scan for the source, but there's too many to know for certain. It could have come from the decapitated body slumped in the curb just there, or the one on the sidewalk, intestines spilling out like dead snakes.

"Shit," I curse and scramble to my feet as I realize for the first time why the street had felt strangely soft. I'm lying on a torso. I have no clue where the limbs wandered off to and have little desire to search them out.

Everything looks red in the pre-dawn light.

Flashes of memory hit me.

The walls of my cell collapse, bowled over by the energy wave erupting from me in a sonic boom. My energy spirals out of me like water down a drain then, suddenly – hunger. *It clamps a fist around my belly and tightens, urging me to chase the most wonderful smell.*

I turn to the newly exposed hallway. My dinner stares back at me, a face so pale I know he won't be enough to sate this twisting, aching need. But a flare of my nostrils calms me slightly. He's not alone.

The memory ends there, and I get a sense of something—the exquisite, coppery taste of blood, though whose I do not know.

Then another memory hits me, sending me to my knee on the sidewalk from its strength.

A narrow set of stairs, freedom in sight. I push open a door, shoving hard enough the lock on the exterior shatters, pieces falling audibly to the floor with a clang. *Above me, the sky is gray, a full moon lighting the world.*

Then, movement near the roof's edge catches my attention as a guard twists toward me. His mouth goes wide with shock, preparing to scream. I don't care if he does. I've traveled up nine floors, and none of the lesser beings had managed to stop me. But my head is pounding and light, whispering voices growing louder with each second, and the half-startled sound he yelps makes them worse.

He isn't loud for long. My fangs, sharper than they've ever been, tear out his throat, his copper-sweet blood filling my mouth. It sates some of the hunger in my belly, but the whispers grow louder.

"Levi," a stranger says from behind me, *"let him go. We can talk about this. You don't need to do this."*

But I realize now, staring blankly at the blood-soaked sidewalk as the memory continues to replay in my head, it wasn't a stranger.

"Aries…" I murmur my friend's name, pain striking me.

All these corpses on the ground, and I hadn't felt guilt until now. I should have, though, shouldn't I? Does it make me a bad person that I just…*hadn't*? Am I even allowed to feel guilty, when I know I'd have done it all over again if I needed to? If the situation repeated and Eryn were in danger again?

But while the dozens of bodies surrounding me hadn't affected me — after all, I hadn't killed all of them, or even most. I can tell from their injuries — the thought that I may have killed Aries haunts me. Is he dead? I don't remember anything after releasing the cooling body. I don't even remember whether the guard had hit the roof or tumbled over the edge.

The look in Aries eyes… I may never forget *that*.

You don't have time for this, my more pragmatic side says, urging me to leave the memories to the past. I know it's right. I need to find Eryn. I lost track of time in the cell and even more time during the bloodlust. I know he's alive — the bond in my chest is still weakly thrumming — but not if he's safe.

Working quickly, I strip myself out of the formerly white prison garb, now ruined. Arterial spray dyed the cloth scarlet, and what looks suspiciously like brain matter clings to the collar. I abandon them on the sidewalk and start hurrying between corpses, stripping them of anything useful I find to clothe myself.

My gaze falls on the corpse half folded into the gutter. *That's a nice jacket…*

Thankfully, the streets are empty of the living, so there's no one to watch me. I find a pair of dark-wash jeans on the corpse of a man dangling partway out of the driver's-side window of a tiny electric car. Somehow, the pants survived their owner's throat being torn out. The jeans fit, but his wingtip shoes are, unfortunately, too small.

Who wears wingtips with jeans? I glare at the man's feet as I shove his body back in the car and keep looking.

Fortunately, I find a pair of motorcycle boots on a dead man two streets over that are close enough.

Combined with the leather jacket I picked off the first body, I'm dressed enough to start my search. I've reached for my bond to Eryn enough times during my imprisonment that it is a simple matter to grasp it now.

It's thin and frail—trying to trace it feels like tracking a spiderweb through a swamp of molasses. The only thing stopping it from snapping is the sheer amount of blood I've gorged myself on.

I can't pinpoint his location exactly, but I *can* feel what direction he's in…north. If I were to go on foot, it would be a day or two's journey, maybe, but luckily, I have other means of travel.

Through the bond, I send my reassurance, then I allow my body to dissolve and my essence to follow the thin, faintly pulsing bond.

Daddy's coming.

I sent it too soon — as soon as I take my ethereal form, I feel it — an insistent, unavoidable pull to the west. I try to resist but find myself caught in its web, tugged along against my will.

And I'm falling into my physical form again but with no memory of choosing to do so. My knees strike the black tar, and an endless presence overwhelms me.

My breath catches in my throat and my head starts to swim as I look up. "Dad?"

* * * *

Pet

That voice.

I know that voice.

I scramble to my feet and turn, my face twisting in horror as my gaze strikes the old wix. Puck is standing in the shifting shadows on the forest's edge. He twitches his arm and I instinctively follow the movement, gasping at the sight of a deadly blade, dripping blood, held in his hand.

"Who... What did you do?" I cry out, jerking forward before I catch myself. What did I think I was going to do? Fight him, unarmed and untrained?

Run, Lily urges, and I wish I could listen to my wolf.

But if I run, will it protect my old pack? Alpha, and my new friends? Or will he just slaughter them in punishment?

If I don't, will he do it anyway?

I stand my ground, my heart racing.

Puck laughs and wipes the bloody blade on his robes. "Were-meat is one of the finest delicacies in the world. Better than calamari or sannakji. There's just something...*powerful* about eating something that's nearly as intelligent as you are. Did you know," the old wix says with a grin, "that you can eat an octopus while it's still alive? Maybe, after I get done cutting that *thing* out of your belly, I should see how *you* taste."

I stumble back a step, heel sinking into the soft dirt of my lily patch, as horror fills me at the thought. "You're insane."

"No, I'm a goddamn *visionary*," he snarls, his anger twisting his face like a funhouse mirror. "Why is it that whenever someone does something a bit *different*, everyone thinks that they're *crazy*?" He moves quicker than a man in his shape should be able to, standing in front of me with his left hand fisted in my sweater before I can back up more than a foot. He lifts the knife in his other hand and presses it to the skin beneath my eye. It burns, and I hold my breath, not daring to flinch.

A silver blade against my skin...

"Hold still," he orders, but I don't want to. I want to run away, but that blade... Could I even move fast enough to avoid it, or would I have to feel it tear into my flesh like paper, spreading its poison through my blood like a wildfire?

My head starts to spin from lack of air, and I try to breathe in without moving. The sound comes out choked, and he just laughs. The blade follows the tracks of my tears down my face, then over the thrumming vein in my neck. Everywhere the silver touches, it burns. I feel the blisters welting on my skin, bringing with them more stinging, saltwater tears.

I'm grateful for my sweater when he gets to my collarbone, a thin armor between the silver and my flesh, but my whole body shudders when he presses the point of the knife harder into my belly. Any more, and it will surely sink in, opening me like a skewer.

"Please," I gasp out, "Please don't do this. There has to be another way, *please*." I cast my mind around for anything, *anything* that might sway him. I land on Daddy. "You...surely you loved Levi once. Killing me will only hurt him, and it won't bring him back to you! But...what if I promise to leave? I'll turn him away if he finds me."

Liar, the little voice in my head accuses me, and I shove it away. This isn't exactly the time to be worried about silly things like *morals*.

"Liar," Puck accuses, and I flinch as if he'd read my mind.

Then I don't care, because with anger in his eyes, he shoves the blade forward. I feel every millimeter as it enters, and I try to flinch away, but his fist is clenched too tight, holding me in place, and my squirming just seems to make the pain worse.

He yanks the blade back out, and I fall to my knees in shock. It just makes it easier for him to plant his bare foot — *Why is it bare? The ground is still white with frost* — on my chest and shove me over, onto my back. The silver is already spreading through my system. I feel my body start to shake without any input from me.

"I hate you," I mumble, folding my hands over my belly and pressing down on the wound. *Is this what shock feels like? This numb, hollow feeling?*

Puck drops down onto my hips, one knee planted on either side, and his weight makes me gag. Still holding the knife in his right hand, he uses his left to grab the collar — *his* collar — still tight around my neck. His nails dig into my flesh as he uses it to yank me up so he can force me to meet his gaze.

"Your feelings for me are irrelevant, little bitch. All that matters is how Daddy feels when he finds your cold, useless body tangled in your own entrails in the dirt." And he drops me and the knife, knocking my hands off my belly so he can dig both of his into the wound.

I scream and clutch at his wrists, trying to yank his hands from my body.

A flock of ravens bursts from a nearby bush, but no one comes to save me.

I am alone.

No one is coming to save me, I know it now. Whether Daddy can't come or just doesn't want to, it no longer matters.

I'm not going to survive this. My wolf is a snarling, snapping beast in my belly, but the silver in my blood has bound them as surely as a chain, and with every twitch of Puck's fingers in my belly, I feel myself fall a little closer to death.

I'm not going to survive this...but he won't either, I decide, and I drop my hand to the dirt. The old wix is too busy with his fumbled search to notice my own — and it takes only a few swipes across the cold ground to reach the hilt of the dagger.

I curl my weak fingers around it and send a prayer to the Goddess Moon. *Give me strength enough for this.*

Then, calmness fills me, like a gift. An answer, I realize, to my prayer. With a steady hand, I take the dagger...and plunge it into Puck's left side, at an upward angle.

Blood sprays from the wound. I don't know if I nicked an artery or his heart, but I realize it doesn't matter.

So does Puck, because his face darkens, even as he bleeds out, and in one last, seemingly desperate move, he fights me for the blade.

I'm not strong enough to hold on, and the last thing I feel is him plunging it into my heart. Then, his body collapses to the side, and the sky above me starts to flicker, darkness coiling across it until my vision goes black.

The world, suddenly, is still.

So am I.

I let go.

Chapter Nineteen

Daddy

"Son," my father says, standing before me for the first time in over an era — and for the first time ever on mortal soil. Already the world seems to have noticed his presence, the sky roiling with black clouds and the ground beneath me quivering.

The Harbinger was never meant to walk this world.

"You never visit, Leviathan, and these are not the circumstances under which I'd hoped our next meeting would occur. Son...what have you done?" Father's voice is a deep rumble, like thunder in the mountains, and each word weighs heavy on my shoulders. I can hear his disappointment.

"Only what was necessary, Father," I admit, shame curling me forward. "He took my bonded."

My father, at least, recognizes what that means. He flinches, his pale skin going bone white. Then, he steps forward — the ground quaking with each footstep and the mortals surrounding us starting to whisper. I feel their fear on the air.

Father places his palm to the side of my neck and closes his eyes. I try to lean into the feeling—it has been so long since I've felt my father's comforting touch, the ice of his skin like a balm to my singed nerves—but find I cannot move, held in place by his will. I sense his presence in my mind as he searches.

"Your bond is frail, Son. Barely a newborn, hardly worth your time," he says after a moment, dropping his hand with a disappointed frown.

A growl pours from my throat, and it's lucky that I cannot move. If I could, I'd have succumbed to my innate need to attack, to punish him for daring to insult my bond. "He is *mine*, father, and the bond will only grow stronger with time," I say instead, the words choked out through gritted teeth.

"You may have had another bonded eventually, if only you'd kept your head. You know what I must to do, Son," Father says, and his apology is clear in his voice. Surely he can't mean…

I turn to ice as I stare at him in horror. "No, Father…you *can't*. I *need* him." Suddenly, my bond with Eryn flares in my chest, growing hot as fire, and I groan, flattening my hand to my sternum.

"Something's wrong…" I mutter to myself, but father still frowns.

"You cannot trick me into changing my mind," he says, but I'm no longer listening.

Even with as weak as our bond is, I can feel Eryn's fear flooding it, stronger than I've ever felt it. He must be terrified. Then, I'm struck by a phantom pain in my chest, strong enough to knock the breath from my lungs.

I meet Father's gaze with horror. "Dad, *please*. He's dying!"

My father's expression goes soft. With it, any hope I was clinging to fades. "I'm sorry, Son. There are rules in place for a reason, and I cannot bend them, not even for you."

"*Please*, Father. Do what you will to me later but let me save him first!" I beg him, tears pouring down my cheeks.

I hadn't expected *this*. I'd expected a censure, maybe—or at worse, that they'd revoke my visa. I'd save Eryn, then spend a few years cooling my heels in Kur while I waited for the paperwork to sort itself out.

But to call my father?

All I'd wanted was to rescue Eryn... Had my actions truly been bad enough to warrant *this*?

"I'm sorry, Son," Father says as he walks around me. He strips me of my jacket, leaving me bare from the waist up.

"Show me your wings," he orders, and no matter how hard I resist, I can't disobey. His voice is an order that none of my kind can ignore. The pain in my chest flares hotter even as my blood-and-bone wings burst free.

Then Eryn's pain is gone—too suddenly to mean anything but death.

My bond to Eryn goes dark and empty, and the absence hurts worse than the pesky damage my father is doing to my body. Bone crunches and dampness coats my skin as he tears off my wings—the very core of my power, my essence. The pain of it is nothing compared to the loss of Eryn.

"Your horns," he orders, and I feel myself drift from my body as it obeys, my mind drowning in the knowledge that I'll never hold my precious little wolf again, never bathe the dirt from his garden off his feet or kiss the smile on his pretty pink lips — never feel our blood bond flourish into the soul bond it was meant to be.

I barely notice him cutting off my horns, leaving throbbing, bony stumps in their place. One step away from being mortal, and soon enough, he takes that too. His hand grows see-through as energy courses through it, and he sinks it in my chest. He takes enough to leave me broken and powerless — but it's not enough.

"All of it," I cry, but he refuses. He leaves behind a kernel of energy, just enough to keep me stuck like this, ageless and everlasting. It's a punishment worse than death.

I scream, the agony finally overwhelming the numbness, but I relish it. I let myself sink into every ounce of suffering until the aching is all that is left and I'm floating in it.

No thoughts.

No memories.

Just pain.

Chapter Twenty

Pet

For an eternity, there is nothing.

Then, there is fire.

It starts in my belly then spreads outward like a spark on dry grass. *The stone,* I realize, just before the pain begins, and I can't think of *anything.* It hurts, worse than anything I've ever felt before — worse than those nights in the mollyhouse, worse than any full moon shift…worse than silver.

My throat is raw, and I realize I'm screaming. I don't know how long it goes on — *what is time, anyway? There's only no-pain and pain, and nothing else* — before I hear voices. Familiar, like I should know them, but thinking is too hard.

I let them gather me up then the world is swaying, and now there is pain *and* nausea. I vomit and someone curses, then someone else says, *"Shit, he's burning up. We need to get him in water."*

Later, as they lower me into an unbearably icy pit, they say, "*It can't be his blood, right? There's not a scratch on him...*" and a flicker of awareness comes to me. It is my blood, right? I remember the dagger in my belly, the biting pain and the surge of silver.

Then another wave of heat, another flood of ice, then something soft. Then nothing, again.

* * * *

I wake up in my bed in the packhouse. The room is too bright, sunlight streaming in from the windows, and I yawn, exhaustion still pulling at my limbs, weighing them down. I try to lift my head, but it's heavy, so I let it fall back to the pillow.

"Eryn?" Alpha Carrick is suddenly leaning over me, his expression concerned.

" —time is it?" I ask around another yawn.

"Almost noon," he answers, hands patting the blankets around me with an awkward sort of movement. "Are you...are you feeling okay?"

"Tired," I answer, rubbing my eyes. "And sore," I add, blinking through the film of sleep. "What happened?"

"We were hoping you could tell us. We found you screaming in the woods —" He keeps talking, but his words open the floodgate of memory.

Puck.

The knife.

The fire.

I flinch, feeling myself go cold. "Is he dead?" I blurt, clutching the blankets as I sit up abruptly, looking around in horror like the old wix is about to step from the shadows.

Alpha is quiet for a second before he asks, "The old man?"

"He's a *monster.*" I fist my hands tighter around the sheets as anger starts to grow. "Is he *dead?*" I need to know.

"Yes. We found his body next to you. We...well, we didn't know what exactly happened, but we figured it wasn't good. We uh...we called the BAA again. The Bureau has agents on their way to pick it up. They'd like to talk to you." Alpha looks uncomfortable as he tells me, but I just sag in relief.

It was self-defense, so I won't get in trouble...right?

I can't change anything that happened, so what's the point in worrying. "Did they say anything about Levi?" I ask hopefully, but Alpha just shakes his head.

"They said they'd explain everything when they got here. Should be within an hour. There's...something else," Alpha adds.

My heart skips a beat and I bite my lip. Alpha stares at me for a second before he smiles and sits on the side of my bed, facing me. "We found another body in the woods."

"Another...Oh Goddess..." My stomach roils at the memory of the bloody knife in Puck's hand. "Who..."

"Beta. They found him shortly after we brought you out of the woods. He...well, it looks like a hunter found him." Alpha doesn't say anything else, but I remember Puck's comments about eating my kind. I scrunch my eyes closed, able to guess exactly what they'd found.

It used to be one of my greatest fears—getting caught in a wolf trap and skinned for my pelt. I might be angry at Beta, but he didn't deserve *that.* "I'm...I'm *sorry,*" I say, a sob choking off the apology.

"It's not your fault, Eryn," Alpha promises, grabbing my hand and squeezing. "It...well, it was a shitty way to go, but he'd have been facing a tribunal anyway. There was never a chance of him making it to the next Goddess Moon. I just wanted you to know."

I nod, mostly so he knows I understand, but I can't help but feel guilty. Will the afterlife still accept his soul if pieces of it have been *eaten*?

I have to hope that the Goddess is forgiving.

More forgiving than me, I think, since part of me is relieved to know the man will never trick me or trap me again.

Alpha sits with me for several long, silent moments until my tears dry, and I feel calmer. Then he says, his voice strained, "Do you feel like you could eat something?"

My stomach rumbles, and I notice for the first time that while the rest of my body feels normal, my stomach still feels warm.

Like a burning coal is nestled somewhere inside, but it's surprisingly comfortable. I press my hand to it and feel a pulse of warmth in return.

Life stone, Lily says, sounding smug, and while I don't understand, I trust them enough to believe that whatever the warmth is, it's not going to harm me.

"I could eat something," I decide, and I'm glad I do, because Alpha looks relieved for the first time since I woke up.

He stands and walks toward the door. "I'll go make you a plate. Stay in bed. I'll be back up." He hesitates with his hand on the knob and says, "Oh, your friends want to check on you. Can I send them in?"

Am I ready for company? I ask myself, and my immediate answer is no. The terror of what Puck

planned to do to me...what he almost succeeded in —
*Did succeed in? How am I still alive? His knife was in my
belly.* I rub my hand over my smooth stomach, not even
a scar to prove my memories true.

Life stone, my wolf says again.

I look back at Alpha and nod. "You can send them
in." I'm not ready to explain, not when I don't have
answers myself, but I don't have the heart to turn them
away. We might not have known each other long, but I
know how I would feel if I was in their shoes.

The two omegas come creeping in as soon as Alpha
leaves, lingering by the door. Three is pale and half
hidden behind Nine, who is staring at me with his jaw
set. "What happened out there?" Nine asks suddenly,
breaking the silence. "You were supposed to be
careful."

His voice breaks, and I understand then that he's not
angry — the anger is just covering up his worry. "I'm
sorry," I apologize, though I know that what happened
wasn't my fault.

"What happened?" Three asks, his voice softer.
"Who was that man?"

I bite my lip, then pat the mattress beside me. "Did I
tell you how I ended up with Dixon?"

They both flinch at his name, and guilt fills me.
Should I avoid his name, or would avoiding what
happened — or acting like it didn't — make it worse?

I don't know, but both Nine and Three join me on
the mattress. Nine sits cross legged near the foot, while
Three grabs a pillow and curls up on his side around it,
staring at me with his wide eyes.

I tell them my story.

* * * *

Rory/Ruari

Of all the streets in the city, how did I stumble on this one? The only one with the man I'm fleeing from standing at the center of it.

I grimace as I stare down at Aries from my perch on the fire escape. Crouched like this, the rickety metal — filled with too many contaminants for the iron to be a concern even for a full-blooded fae, of which I am definitely *not* — is as good as a wall at keeping me from sight.

He's faced off with a naked woman. His hands are empty and outstretched. He's dodging and weaving, avoiding each attempted hit but not attempting to fight back. I jolt when I remember that, in my pique, I took his weapons, and whoever he's facing *is* a weapon.

Cursing, I leap over the railing of the fire escape, landing silently on the balls of my feet on the sidewalk below.

Not quite enough to avoid notice, apparently. The naked woman spins toward me with a hiss, her hands lifted. Deadly sharp claws top each finger, black and oozing something I suspect is poison.

Venom?

I've never known the difference and now, I realize as she springs toward me, is not the time to figure it out. I dodge back, narrowly avoiding a swipe of her claws.

Maybe jumping in was a bad idea? I snark at myself.

Shut up, I bite back, ducking under her next attack but not fast enough. The tip of a claw skims over my forehead, and I hiss at the burn.

"Bitch!" I say with a yelp, jumping backward to clutch at my head. It's a bad idea, since now the sticky, burning fluid is on my hand. "The fuck is this nasty?"

"Never felt a woman's pleasure before?" she purrs, dipping her hand between her thighs to coat it again with the fluid.

A succubus... Crap.

"Oh...oh, gross." I shudder and wipe my hand on my pants—and in doing so, I feel the hilt of Aries' dagger. Yanking it out with little care, I chuck it toward Aries. It flies through the air, narrowly missing the succubus, and she laughs.

"Missed me," she taunts, then she leaps toward me.

"As *if*," I snap back, since I'd have hit her for sure if I was aiming at her.

Then Aries groans, and I know I've proven my point. I didn't even intend to hit him, and look! The blade is stuck in his biceps like it's a perfect fleshy scabbard.

He pulls it out, and I watch, sickly fascinated, by the way it emerges, all coated in shiny red stuff. "Oops?" I say, then remember I'm in the middle of something arguably more important—to *some* people at least—as the succubus catches me again with her claws.

This time, she clamps her hands around my neck, her nails biting into my skin, and I yelp at the sting. "A little help," I holler—or try to—but she's cut off my breath, and all that emerges is a choked whine. I've fought human vagrants and fae warriors and things in between, but never a demon. Never something like *me*.

Then the tip of a dagger emerges from *her* throat, and she lets me fall, her claws scrabbling at her neck as she gurgles around it. I stand up and brush the dirt—okay, and blood and guts and possibly a bit of brain matter—off my ass.

"Well, that worked out just fine," I say after a second, staring down at the demon while the light leaves her eyes — except...I lean down and glare at her. She's still alive, gasping around the knife. "She's not dying..." I point out.

He ignores me to pull out the blade, wiping it on his pants before he returns it to his scabbard. The one on his waist, not the new hole in his arm, which appears to no longer be bleeding. Instead, he glares at me as he fishes out his handcuffs and flips the succubus over to cuff her.

"You following me?" he asks, as if I hadn't just distracted the woman and, you know, saved his *life*.

"That's really what you're worried about?" I ask, lifting a brow and pasting on a smile. All I really want is to slink away and lick my wounds in private — the metaphorical wounds, at least. The way he looks at me...one would think that *I* had hurt *him*, and not the other way around!

"Ruari — Rory," he corrects himself to the anglicized pronunciation as soon as I glare at him. "I'm serious. Were you following me?"

"What do you care? Besides, I have better things to do than follow *you* around." I cross my arms. It's probably true... I'm sure I *could* find something else to do. I mean, so what if I was just smoking a joint on the fire escape? The streets don't seem particularly safe at the moment, so there didn't seem to be much reason to be walking them.

Unless, apparently, one is a faerie prince.

"Look. I have to get her back to headqu — to camp." He stumbles over the word and for a second, I feel bad for him. I'd run into a few of the other unhoused after leaving the squat and gathered enough information for them to string together what happened.

Something—many *somethings*—escaped from the BAA prison cells and were running amok in the city. Most of the people, after passing on the information, had urged me to find somewhere to bunker down, but there seemed little point.

I'd been trying to die since my spell backfired, trapping me in this cursed, not-quite-human body. Every time, though, the monster now living inside me pops out like a jack-in-a-box and stays my hand.

"I'm not stopping you," I tell him, after he stares at me for an uncomfortably long time without adding anything else. "It's that way." I gesture to the west, just in case he hadn't figured it out yet.

"No, I know, just… Look. It's dangerous out here—" he starts to say, and I immediately roll my eyes.

He's certainly not concerned about *my* well-being now, after all these years, and he's already seen how little help I am in a fight. "What? You want me to watch your back?" I interrupt.

"No," he answers, so quickly that I'm pretty sure I should be offended. "I mean, *yes*, but I want to watch yours, too. Come with me."

"Pass." I turn on my heel and start to walk back toward my squat. After a second, he curses and the succubus shrieks, loud enough I can't help but turn and look. He has her draped over his shoulder like a sack of potatoes, and he's running after me. Every step he takes, she bounces up and down.

I laugh when I realize that each one of his steps causes her large, balloon-esque breasts to flop around and slap him on the back. The sound is reminiscent of someone in flipflops.

"Hold up," he calls, and for a second, I consider listening.

Then I remember all the pain he put me through — and all the pain I endured after he abandoned me to *her* — and I speed up instead. "See you in another life," I call back, darting around the next corner and into an alley that, at first glance, appears to be a dead end.

But I know these streets like the back of my hand. A leap and a twist, and I'm on the ladder to the fire escape, then it's as simple as ducking into an unlocked window, and I've lost him.

* * * *

Princeling

I stare at the fire escape that Rory just darted up, agile as a fucking cat, and know there's no way to follow, not without leaving the succubus behind. And she may be contained now, but the magic of the cuffs will wear off sooner or later, then she'll be free to terrorize the city again.

"Shit!" I curse, then spin on my heel. I just have to hope that Rory will be fine on his own.

Why do I even care? I wonder, and the thought spins around like a stationary bike in my mind. After the way he disappeared on me before, should I be surprised that he'd do the same now?

Shoulders slumped — as much as they can be, with the demon over one — I turn and trudge back to the street. I can't force him to safety now any more than I could then.

It takes me a mile of walking through the city to find a way out of it — a horse, still attached to a broken-down buggy and by some miracle, still alive. The beast knickers when it sees me, straining against its harness to reach me. I don't know if it—he, I realize when I get close enough—senses my *sidhe* nature, or if he's just as desperate to get out of the city as I am.

In the end, it doesn't matter. I take a moment stroking his neck, calming him down until his eyes are no longer rolling, then I unhook him from the buggy. I don't need the reins, so I remove them from his bridle and use them to tie the pissed off succubus into a bundle that's less likely to spook him.

Then, I throw her now-bound form over his back before I climb up after. It's been a while since I've ridden, especially bareback, but the knowledge floods back to me immediately.

"Good boy," I murmur as he takes off at a trot, obeying each nudge of my knees. I lean forward and let my fingers tangle in his mane as he quickens his pace. The sound of his hooves on the sidewalk is strange, nothing like riding through the meadows of my youth, but the feel of his muscles bunching under my thighs is achingly familiar.

Everything seems to be going perfectly—until the demon starts to scream.

Then she melts away, her body dripping like candlewax off the horse and disappearing into thin air. The horse startles at the weight change, and I'm lucky he doesn't buck me, but by the time he stands still…the succubus is gone, no trace of her left.

Chapter Twenty-One

Pet

Old York is a scarlet stain on the horizon, dark even under the noon sun, and I shiver as I stare at the ruins. "What happened?" I ask in horror, unable to pull my gaze away.

The agent who escorted me here from Havenwood Pack, Agent Shaw, gives me a look of pity but doesn't answer. Instead, he nods at me to keep walking and says, "Come on. They're waiting for you."

"They?" I blurt, the fear of what's coming finally enough to drag my attention from the smoke.

"I'm not at liberty to disclose any information," he intones dryly. He doesn't seem nervous, but then again...why would he? Whoever 'they' are that he's taking me to, they won't do anything to him. He's just the delivery boy.

Agent Shaw stumbles a bit, then glances back at me, expression wry. "I'm not *just* a delivery boy, Eryn. I'm also a telepath. You don't need to worry. You're not in trouble."

Heat burns my cheeks as I realize he's in my head, and I didn't even know it. Then I go cold as I wonder what *else* he sees. Are all my secrets—my worst memories, the time with Dixon...are they all there, on display?

"Just what's actively crossing your mind," he answers my unspoken question with a gentle smile. "You need to be thinking of it for me to hear it. I'd shut you out if I could, trust me, but it's not something that just turns off."

"That must be terrible," I say, once my initial worry fades. Hearing everything that everyone around you was thinking, all the time? I can't imagine it.

"It has its downsides. Here we are," he says, changing the topic abruptly as we come to a halt outside the front door of...

"A bank?" I blurt, surprised, as I stare at the face of the building.

"Headquarters, for now at least," he explains, flashing his badge at an agent waiting on the other side of the glass door. The other man examines it closely before a buzzer sounds and the door unlocks.

Agent Shaw holds it open, gesturing for me to go inside first, and filled with reluctance, I do. I don't know what I expect, but it looks...normal. There is no makeshift triage unit in the lobby or crying people huddled in corners—just a typical bank, like any other bank I'd ever seen in a holo.

Agent Shaw pushes the button to the left of a pair of silver, sliding doors. *An elevator*, I realize as they slide open. He follows me inside, and we ride it up to the third floor.

Anxiety is still twisting in my belly, and the life stone pulses like it's trying to reassure me. It helps a little, though I don't know if it will protect me a second time. Still, I curl my hand reassuringly over its heat.

Beside me, Agent Shaw makes a choked sound, and when I look at him, he's staring at me in shock.

"What? What's wrong?" I ask, my anxiety spiking.

He clears his throat and shakes his head. "Nothing, nothing."

The elevator doors slide open with a *ding* before I can question him further, and he walks out immediately...like he doesn't *want* me to question him further, I realize. Biting my lip, I debate letting the doors close and riding the elevator back down...trying to escape before whoever is waiting for me here sees me.

But I need to know what happened to Levi, and these are the only people who can tell me.

"You can do this," I mutter to myself, and clench my fists. "You escaped the warehouse, and Dixon. You escaped Puck." I try not to think the word *killed,* but it crosses my mind anyway, and I lock a worried gaze on Agent Shaw, who just looks back at me with an arched brow before he gestures toward a closed door.

"Are you coming, Eryn?"

* * * *

Daddy

Why couldn't my father have broken my mind when he shattered my body?

I've had the thought dozens of times since the two agents carried my limp, barely conscious body into this room. They'd been gentle—far kinder than they needed to be—as they placed me on the twin mattress against the wall. They could have stuck me in a jail cell to rot, but it seemed someone in the BAA thought I'd been punished enough.

Losing Eryn was worse than anything they'd done to me.

How could I care that when I reach for that core of energy in my chest, all I feel is emptiness? I keep hearing my father's words—*"I disown you, Leviathan, Son of None. Kur has forsaken you to the mortal coil. May you live the remainder of your life in peace, for you will not be welcomed home."*

Not only had I lost Eryn, but I'd lost my family, too. He hadn't had the decency to take everything, though.

I could still feel that tiny spark of *ether* at my core, taunting me with the knowledge that even without my wings and horns and my magic siphoned out, he'd left me my lifespan.

Long and empty—and doomed to be alone.

Couldn't he have killed me?

Or at least done to me what he'd done to the rest of the demons who'd escaped? I'd been barely conscious, but I'd watched him summon the rest, then banish them to Kur for their punishment.

At least while being tortured, you weren't alone. Besides, I deserved to suffer. I'd promised my boy I'd keep him safe, and now he's gone…and it's all my fault.

The hinges whine as someone cracks open the door, but I don't bother turning to look. I don't care who it is, unless they are here to kill me, in which case I'd say go ahead.

"Go away," I growl after a stretch of time passes, and no one has tried to kill me.

"Oh, really now, Master Levi," a familiar voice huffs, and Maggie has rounded the bed to face me. She glares down at me, her hair a fiery wild mess around her disapproving face. "Is this what Eryn wants? A moping, miserable fool for a master?"

"It doesn't matter what he wants," I snarl, rolling to my other side and yanking my pillow over my face.

I can't say the rest. *It doesn't matter what he wants, because he's dead.*

I can't force myself to face the truth.

"Oh, it doesn't? And here I was thinking you'd say it was the *only* thing that matters." Suddenly, something hits me — the other pillow, maybe? — and she says, voice sharp, "Up. Get up, Master Levi, or I shall be forced to find a bucket of ice water."

"What's it matter, Maggie? What does *anything* matter?" I uncover my face and flop onto my back. My body feels so weak now, without my magic flooding it.

"I didn't portal in all the way from Brekkan — and you know how much I hate to portal, Leviathan — to listen to you mope and whine while your boy sits in a conference room down the hall getting interrogated by small-minded federal agents about your mental state!"

"My — What on *earth* are you going on about, woman?" I finally cave and stare at her with exasperation. "Eryn *died*. I felt it."

"Well, clearly, you felt wrong, because he's alive and kicking, and looking very much like a boy in need of his Daddy — *not* the miserable wretch of a creature I'm staring at now." Maggie barely finishes speaking before I roll out of bed and start for the door, on a mission to find him.

If he's alive…if he's really here…

"Your clothing, Leviathan!" she hollers after me, but I couldn't give two shits what I'm wearing, or not wearing in this case. I'm far from nude. The dirty, torn jeans cover enough of my body that I'm not breaking any laws. I'm not wasting a single second more for something as banal as a wardrobe change.

I do realize once I'm in the hallway, however, that I have no idea where I'm supposed to go. Abruptly, I halt, then spin on my heel to stare at Maggie. "Where?" I demand, and thankfully, she knows exactly what I'm asking.

"Third door on the left, that way." She points, and I spin around, storming toward it. I shove it open with a clatter, ignoring the agent standing outside's protest. It takes more effort than I'm used to, and I feel slightly out of breath as I race inside.

I refuse to let this stupid mortality slow me down. "Eryn?" I look around and relief slams into me as I spot him, weakening my knees. I stumble, planting my palm on the doorframe to steady myself. "Baby…" I breathe.

Eryn turns his face to me as soon as I speak, then he's up and running toward me, practically leaping into my arms. I catch him with a choked laugh. "Oh gods, sweetheart, I thought…"

"Daddy!" he cries, clinging to me even tighter, his own voice breaking on a sob. I can feel him shaking and hold him closer. I hate to think what he may have gone through. "I was so worried about you," he adds, his voice muffled as he buries his face against my neck, his breath warm.

After everything, he's worried about me? He's too sweet for his own good. "I'm fine, baby," I lie. I'm not fine, not yet. But now that Eryn is back in my arms, maybe I will be. I loosen my hold slightly, nudging him back just enough that I can stare at his face, taking in every minuscule detail, from the damp eyelashes to the little lines around his mouth — like he's been frowning.

"How...how are you here, baby? I felt..." I hesitate, then place my left hand on his chest, over his heart, feeling the reassuring beat. Strong, and steady. "I *thought* I felt you die."

"We were wondering the same thing." A stranger interrupts us, and I turn to him with a scowl.

"Excuse me?" I'm still not used to this new disrespect I've been on the receiving end of ever since I woke up on the sidewalk in front of my father, weak and powerless. I don't know if it's the lack of fear now that I can't kill them with a look, or if it's the loss of my titles, but either way, I hate it.

Will Eryn even still want me now?

"We were in the middle of an interview, and we have limited time, so if you don't mind?" The agent, a werewolf I don't recognize, gestures back toward the chair Eryn had been sitting in before my entrance.

"From what I heard, you were in the middle of an interrogation," I grumble, refusing to let Eryn go. I narrow my eyes at the man. "But I'm sure that's not true, because Eryn hasn't done anything wrong. Isn't that right, Agent...?" I trail off, waiting for a name.

To be fair, I don't know everything that he's been up to since Puck stole him from me, but I know Eryn, and I know he wouldn't have done anything to warrant being treated like a criminal.

"Agent Simmons. And of course he hasn't. We just need to get his statement. *You* are supposed to be resting. Your father said —"

"I can rest here just as well as anywhere else," I decide. I try to pick Eryn up but groan when my arms start to shake. He's not even that heavy, skinnier now than he was before, which is saying something, but my muscles aren't used to working without the blood energy coursing through my veins.

Instead of carrying him, I pull Eryn close to my side and walk with him, and when we get to the armchair, I sit down and tug him into my lap. He doesn't protest the closeness. He snuggles in even closer, sitting sideways and pulling his feet up onto the cushion just to the right of my thighs, knees tucked to our chest.

I rub my face over his hair, breathing in his scent. It's subtle but there, buried underneath the odor of cheap shampoo and wolves—men that aren't me. A growl rumbles in my throat, and I force it down as soon as I hear Eryn whimper.

"Where were we?" Agent Simmons asks as he sits in the chair opposite us, picking up a notebook and pen off the end table beside him. He flips it open and looks back at us.

"I...I was telling you about D-Di—" Eryn stumbles over his words, his voice shaking, and I take his hand, squeezing it.

"I'm right here, sweetheart. I won't let anyone hurt you again." I promise, even though it's one I know I can't keep—not anymore, not like *this*, little better than a blank.

"I just..." Eryn peers up at me, his concern evident. "I don't want you to be angry with me for..."

"Nothing, sweetheart. There's nothing you're going to say that will make me angry with you. If you did something, I trust that it was because you had no choice." I tip his face up a bit more so I can meet his eyes. "I love you, Eryn. Nothing is going to change that. I promise."

Chapter Twenty-Two

Rory/Ruari

The unlocked window opens into a tiny apartment, the front door barely two skips and a hop away. It's wide open, like whoever lived here had run out in a hurry and never bothered to close it. It's a testament to the sheer amount of panic that flooded the city last night that all their belongings are still accounted for.

A quick peek through the window to the fire escape shows that Aries has given up his pursuit. I can see him walking away. I'm happy about that, for sure. There *definitely* isn't a small part of me disappointed that he's let me leave again. That I'm staring at his back as he's walked away, again.

I kick the wall beneath the window and hold my breath until the urge to scream fades, then turn around.

"Well," I say out loud, glancing at the empty apartment. Though, it's not quite empty...not yet. Something sparkly catches my eye from the little table next to the worn armchair. "Ooh, shiny." I pick up the necklace. It's a cheap thing, all plastic beads and thread, but I like it, so I string it around my neck.

I flutter through the rest of the apartment, stuffing my pockets as I go. I leave the cash — what use do I have for paper? — but like a magpie, I gather anything shiny I can find. A ring for this finger, a silver clip for my hair.

I pick up a spoon — tarnished, but it has potential. I hold it up to the light but then my eyes go blurry, the ceiling seeming to stretch further and further away…until I realize it's not moving.

I am.

My hands go numb, the spoon falling through my skin like I'm made out of pudding, and that's when I feel it. A calling, irresistible — impossible to ignore, like a fishhook just sank into the skin behind my belly button and pinched, and now I'm being dragged along behind it.

The world turns to liquid, and I can't breathe as I fall below it, like a stone sinking in a lake. My mouth opens and closes, but just as I grow lightheaded, blackness curling around the edges of my vision, a heavy weight wraps around me and drags me back up to the surface.

I fall to my knees onto hard, hot asphalt, gagging at the taste of rotten eggs that appears on my tongue. I suck in a breath, oxygen filling my lungs so quickly I worry they'll explode.

The image dances in my brain — a pair of overinflated lungs bursting, spilling scarlet blood onto the ground like a pollock painting.

"Who are you, little one? You're not one of mine…" A deep voice, strange and unfamiliar, is the first thing I hear.

I force my eyes open — *when had I shut them?* — and see a large man.

Well, a large being. I can immediately tell that whoever he is, 'man' is an inadequate modifier. He's seven feet tall if he's an inch, with skin as white as fresh fallen snow. Even his hair is white, growing like a horse's mane along the top of his head. The sides are smooth, no stubble to be seen. And his eyes…? They are cerulean blue and endless.

I feel like I'm staring into a lake with no bottom.

I draw in another breath, preparing myself to ask who *he* is, and what he means when he says that I'm not one of his, when a new voice stops me cold.

"No. He's one of *mine*."

No. She can't be here.

Like a lodestone, her very presence draws my gaze, and a whine spills out of my mouth unbidden.

She looks exactly like she did in my memories.

Queen Nuala.

The woman who raised me, fed me honeysuckle water and clover from her own garden — the woman who stole me from the arms of my mother as a babe, leaving behind a bundle of charmed sticks in my place.

Some mornings, I still wonder what that woman thought when three days later, she went to pick up her child in the morning and found a marionette in my place. Did she grieve?

Fear grips me tight as Queen Nuala rests her gaze on my kneeling form. Her smile is sharp and cutting.

Memory leaks from the poorly patched walls I'd shoved them behind.

Cat-o-nine's lashing the skin from my back.

Salt packed in the wounds.

Chanting and screeching, rituals born from my blood and pain.

"Stop!" I holler, slapping my hands to my ears and scrunching my eyes closed, as if dulling my senses will in some way make her go away.

It does nothing — absolutely nothing — to prevent me from hearing her laugh, a thing made of brambles and gravel.

"My little lost bird," she purrs, each of her footsteps like an earthquake as she approaches me and the stranger. "Finally returned to the nest. Thank you, Harbinger. I'll take him home."

I try to open my mouth in protest, but I can't. I don't know how she's done it — cast a spell with nary a sound or movement — but I'm frozen in place. A statue for her taking.

Inwardly, I start to scream.

No one hears me.

* * * *

Pet

Telling my story to Agent Simmons is even harder with Daddy in the room. I love the feeling of his arms around me, like a safety blanket protecting me from all the evils of the world, but I don't want him to know what I went through. I don't want that to be the only thing he sees when he looks at me. I don't want him to think of that when we…

If we…

I swallow and push the thought away for now to concentrate on giving my statement. I try to go light on some of the details — especially about those days locked up in the mollyhouse — but the agent keeps pressing, asking question after question, until I've given him almost every detail.

Daddy growls a few times and tightens his arms around me more than once, but he stays quiet and not once does he turn his anger on me. When I'm finished, my mouth is dry, and I'm grateful for the water Agent Simmons offers. I suspect, from the look on his face and the way he keeps shifting his weight toward the door, that he asked just for a chance to leave the room for a second, but I'm grateful anyway.

As soon as the agent leaves, Daddy shifts me off his lap. "Stand up for me," he says, and while he doesn't sound angry, my gratitude dies a quick death, replaced by fear. Is this when he tells me I'm not allowed to go home with him now that we are alone? Was he just waiting to not have an audience?

I scramble, still obedient even at the last, to my feet, wringing my hands as I stare at him, waiting for him to say it. I scan his face for every small detail, trying to memorize it, but tears still turn him into a blur.

"No, no, don't cry, sweetheart," he says in a voice that, if I didn't know better, I'd say was begging. Then, he shifts forward to perch at the edge of the chair and lifts his hands to cup my face. His fingers swipe away my tears. "I just want to look at you, need to make sure you're okay."

"You…you're not going to send me away?" I ask in a warbling voice, and Daddy's expression falls with horror.

"Of course not," he says, his voice sharp, but this time I don't flinch. He's not mad at me. He's mad at the idea of me being gone…and it helps soothe the rough edges of my fear. He plants his hand, palm flat, over my heart, as if he needs to feel it. "I know you said you're fine...that you told the agent that you're okay...but I need to see it with my own eyes."

"Me, too," I agree, my chin wobbling. "I saw Puck stab you and...and..." I sniff back another round of tears before I continue. "I didn't know if you were alive or dead."

"It would take more than that to keep me from you, baby," he promises. Then, he drifts his hands to the top button of my shirt, hesitating over the small round piece of plastic. "May I?"

Immediately, I nod. As long as he's planning on keeping me, I'll let him do anything, absolutely anything, that he wants. Quickly, he works each button free, then spreads my shirt open, exposing my pale, bare chest to his gaze.

There's not even a scar where Puck stabbed me.

He presses his hand to my bare skin like he's feeling for my heartbeat. "I can feel it," he breathes out, the sound shaky. "Warm and pulsing, like your heartbeat is echoing. The stone... What did it look like?"

I shiver under his touch but try to remember. "I didn't really see it," I finally give up and admit, ashamed that I can't answer him. "I'm sorry."

"Don't apologize. I was just curious." Daddy smiles at me and leans forward, pressing his lips in a kiss to the bottom of my breastbone. His mouth is soft and warm, then his hair falls forward, tickling my skin.

When he sits back, his gaze drifts higher and he frowns, lifting his hands to touch the iron collar still stuck around my neck. "I want this off. The only collar you should be wearing is mine."

"Agent Simmons promised they'd send someone in to look at it as soon as I was done here," I reply, lifting my own hand to the stupid collar. Sometimes, I can forget it's there, but others, like now...it's a reminder of everything that happened.

Of Puck taking me from Daddy and breaking his pretty gold collar, the one that proved I belonged to him. Of Puck's threats as he snapped this one around my neck...of Dixon's hands, gripping it at the back as he...

I shudder and Daddy moves quickly to tug me into his lap again. He doesn't rebutton my shirt and I don't bother to, either. Instead, I just settle in closer. He runs his left hand up and down my chest, like he can't bear the thought of not touching me. It's soothing, chasing away the bad memories.

Finally, my brain seems to come back online, and I'm able to ignore his touch enough to say, "What do you think happened to the weapon?" I can't remember what the old wix called it, just that it was a foreign name that sat oddly on his tongue, but he'd claimed it could kill death.

Never dying sounded like a dream—always being with Daddy and never having to worry about it ending—but I'm not stupid enough to think it would end well. Even if there were no more diseases, no more war or violence...eventually, over-population would be an issue. So no one could starve to death... That wouldn't stop the starving people from suffering.

I shiver at the thought. Being perpetually hungry with no hopes of an ending, not even one as tragic as death? It sounds like a horror story.

"No one will tell me anything, for obvious reasons," Levi adds, stilling his hand on my skin for a second before he seems to gather himself, "but if I had to guess, I'd say whatever pieces Puck managed to assemble have been taken apart and stored somewhere safe—a bank vault or a museum. I doubt there's much left of the BAA headquarters at the moment."

I look up at Daddy's face just in time to see him flinch, his shame easy to read. This time, it's my turn to comfort him. I lift my hand to his face, tracing my fingers over his frown lines. "You did what you had to, right?" I say, and it comes out like a question.

"There was no other way," he mutters, but I can tell he's not certain.

So, I say it again for him, infusing the words with every bit of confidence and reassurance that I can. "There was no other way." I know Levi, and I know my Daddy wouldn't have killed anyone if he had a choice. I remember the way he fretted over me after that first day in the cell when he'd nearly drained me.

That wasn't the behavior of someone who didn't care.

Daddy doesn't look convinced, but before I can say anything else, Agent Simmons raps on the door and walks inside. He hands me a sealed bottle of water. I accept it with a whispered, "Thank you," and crack open the lid, taking a small sip.

"No need to thank me. How…" Agent Simmons shifts his gaze from me—specifically, my bare chest, fully on display—to Daddy, looking uncomfortable. "How long will you be staying?"

Daddy pets his hands along my skin in a soothing back and forth motion, tracing invisible patterns on my skin. "That depends, doesn't it? How soon are we allowed to leave?"

Agent Simmons swallows, and I hold my breath while I wait for an answer. I don't know the full story — for some reason, every time I've asked when I could see Levi, and whether he was okay, and where was he, people stutter and walk away like the floor just turned to lava beneath their feet.

I'm not stupid, though. I've heard people whispering, and I know he had something to do with a number of deaths in the city. A *large* number of deaths.

Should I be scared of him? Or…or angry?

Maybe, but if I'd had the power to—if I were anything but a half-broken werewolf at the time—I'd have done whatever it took to save Levi back at the hotel, even if it meant others would die.

I move my hand until I can grab Daddy's and lace our fingers together. I meant what I told him a few seconds ago. I truly believe that if he'd had another choice, he would have taken it. I'll just have to believe it hard enough for both of us.

Agent Simmons clears his throat. "The Council…has decided to abide by your father's ruling. You'll be free to return to your estate in Brekkan, provided there are no further…incidents."

Levi is quiet for a few seconds, then he tips his head down in acknowledgment. "There will be no further incidents." He shifts beneath me, then adds, "What of our things from the hotel?"

"Held for evidence. They'll be shipped to your home when they're released," Agent Simmons answers, but there's something in his voice that makes me think he's really saying *if*, not *when*.

Daddy sighs. "I suppose I don't need it anymore, do I?" Then, he looks at me, quirking his lips up in a smile. "Ready to go home, darling?"

"Please, yes," I agree.

"Is there someone who can come take care of this?" Daddy says to the agent, tapping the iron collar around my neck at the same time.

"He's waiting in the hallway. I can send him in now." Agent Simmons turns sharply on his heel and walks to the door, ushering in a second agent. This one is older, his hair gone white. His hands are crooked and wrinkled but he makes quick work of the collar.

In seconds, it opens with a loud click. It feels like the weight of a mountain is lifted off my shoulders as he pulls it away. "Would you like to keep it?" The man asks, but both Daddy and I blurt our answer at the same time.

"No," we both agree, and I can't even force myself to watch as the man shrugs and carries it out of the room. I feel like I don't relax again until I hear the door shut. Then, I lift my hand to my neck, testing my skin as if to make sure it's really gone.

Daddy covers my hand with his. "Better?" he asks.

I shrug. "I feel...bare." I miss wearing Daddy's collar.

"Collar or no collar...you are mine, Eryn. You belong to me, now and always," Daddy promises.

Maybe that should make me feel lesser, like property. Maybe someone else would be offended or upset. Me?

I feel relieved.

"Now and always," I repeat, voice quieter as I say it to myself. Then, I smile.

Chapter Twenty-Three

Daddy

"Isn't there someone who could open a portal?" I ask, staring at the dinky little buggy and mule waiting on the street.

The agent frowns, judgment leaking from his pores. "Anyone capable of doing that is a bit busy in the city."

I huff and consider raising a stink, but at the last moment I hesitate. I'm no longer a prince. My name has no authority now. I can't issue threats. I'm powerless to follow through on them.

I can't even intimidate him with my physical prowess. Walking down the stairs to the ground floor left me out of breath. How do blanks do this day in and day out?

"It's fine, D— Levi." Eryn lays his hand on my arm, and the skin-to-skin contact immediately helps me calm down.

I turn to the office, about to ask if we could at least take a plane, when Eryn brightens. "It'll be just like a road trip!"

How can I disappoint him when he's looking at me like that? I reach up and tuck a few strands of his hair — gods, it's gotten longer — behind his ear, letting my fingers linger on his skin.

"Should we get road snacks?" I ask, and while part of me is teasing, the way Eryn is beaming is worth sending Maggie out to grab some. Then Eryn turns to look at something — I don't know what, I can't take my eyes off him long enough to figure it out — and the move leaves his neck bare.

Hunger stirs in my belly for the first time since I woke on the street. Until now, a small part of me had started to wonder if my father, despite his promise, had left me fully mortal after all.

Eryn, Maggie and I load up into the buggy. I keep my head high, despite the indignity of riding in something so far below my status. *Previous* status, I remind myself. At least the BAA provided a driver for us — though I suspect that is due to their desire to ensure I end up back at my estate like I'm supposed to.

I find myself staring at my boy, the way he's bouncing on the hard wooden bench, face pressed to the yellowed glass, and I smile.

It's worth it.

All of this is worth it if it means I get to keep him.

Eryn flags a few hours in, his overabundance of excitement dulling as the newness fades. As soon as he starts to wince, I slide back on my bench — even though it leaves an awful kink in my back — and encourage him onto my lap. He immediately settles down with a relieved sigh, and now it's my turn to wince. Thankfully, with the way he's seated, he doesn't notice.

I wrap my arms around his waist to help hold him in place as he lays his head against my chest. His right hand lands, as if by accident, against my chest, his palm flat over my nipple.

I wish it was his mouth.

As if she can sense where my mind is headed — and who knows, maybe she can? It would certainly explain how she's managed to run my estate so effectively, despite being only human — Maggie clears her throat. "As cute as you two are, I'd ask that you remember that you aren't alone in this buggy, Master Levi."

Eryn startles, looking up at me with an embarrassed stare that has me grinning. Without breaking eye contact with him, I say to her, "One would have to be both blind and deaf to miss you, my darling."

"One would have to both blind, deaf and dumb, I'd think — by which I mean, quite stupid. After all, without me, you'd still be wallowing in bed like a scolded schoolboy," Maggie says, voice dry but laced with humor.

"You may have a point," I admit.

"Daddy?" Eryn says, interrupting, and I love the way his cheeks turn pink, the color spreading down his neck. I trace the color with my fingertips, lingering over his strong, steady pulse. There's no better proof of life than the feeling of his blood in his veins, coursing under my fingers.

"Yes, sweetheart?" I finally say, after the seconds stretch too long without him speaking.

"You seem...different. Are you okay? Is it because of what Puck did?" He speaks quietly and his voice stumbles on Puck's name, but I'm proud of him for being brave enough to ask, even if I hate having to answer.

I will never lie to him, though.

"I *am* different, but it's not because of what Puck did. What I did to escape...? Well, it broke one of the most fundamental laws of my kind. Despite what the humans" — I spit the word like a curse — "think in their silly little Bible, my kind are not evil, not innately. We serve a grander purpose. Our magic is not meant to be unleashed like mine was, and doing so... It has consequences."

"Consequences?" Eryn repeats, and I can sense his worry.

I skim my fingers over his lips, tickling the corner until it twitches into a smile, albeit a small one. "My father disavowed me. It's like being disinherited, but...more. He stripped me of my ability to reach the ether. I'm not fully mortal. I still need to feed" — I lower my hand to his neck again, petting over his thrumming veins — "and I still won't age. I just also don't have the strength or...magic, for lack of a better word, that I did before."

Eryn bites his lower lip and I *tsk,* tugging it free. He sucks in a breath, the sound a bit ragged, and I worry.

Without my magic and name, will he still want me?

But then he asks, "Does it hurt?" and I realize he's not upset because he thinks I'm now lesser, but because he cares — about me, not my name. Not about what I can give him or do for him, but just...me.

"Not at all, sweetheart," I lie, because any pain I feel, the hollow aching at my core that won't quite go away, is worth it to be here with him now.

Then he smiles, and I know that I made the right choice. "Go to sleep, sweetheart," I murmur when he yawns. "I'll watch over you."

By the time the buggy trundles to a stop several hours later, even Eryn looks worn out. Maggie's curls are hanging limp, and partway through the day she'd dragged a blanket out of her handbag to drape over her shoulders. She'd pulled a second one out for Eryn shortly after he woke. It was small and green, the perfect size for his lap.

I'd cleared my throat and asked where mine was, and she'd had the audacity to smirk at me and say, "Darling, it's wherever you packed it."

She knows damn well I hadn't packed anything.

But since her expression had basically dared me to do anything but sit back and smile, I'd held my tongue. Eryn, the sweetheart, had just scooched closer and draped half of his blanket over my thighs, blinking up at me with a small smile. "I'll share, Daddy."

The driver bangs on the door. "Out you get. I need to stable Betsy." With a bit of grumbling, the three of us stumble out onto the sidewalk. I stretch, my back cracking painfully, and Eryn groans as he bends forward, his hands planted on his hips. Even Maggie is wincing as she rubs her ass with her left hand.

The driver swings back up onto the front bench, and with a swish of the reins, he goads the mule into a slow trot around the side of the squat building. Eryn sidles closer to me, clinging to my side. "Is this a hotel?" he asks.

"I suppose one could call it that," I say, scrunching my nose as I stare at it. I would personally prefer the word 'hovel'.

"It's certainly...colorful," Maggie says, and her voice is hesitant, like she had to struggle to think of something nice to say. She's not wrong, though. The siding is a garish yellow, and the shingled roof is red, but the shutters beside the windows are forest green. The front door is blue.

At least the Bureau booked us two rooms.

* * * *

Pet

Daddy looks...different.

Not in a bad way, though. He's as handsome as ever, and just looking at him has me craving his touch. He just seems a bit softer, more human. Approachable, maybe? I don't feel as much like I don't belong.

Maybe it's because of what his father did — or maybe it's me that's changed. I survived Whisper and Puck and Dixon, and even helped rescue the other omegas. They'd chosen to stay behind at Havenwood, but I'd promised Alpha I'd try to come back and visit.

Whatever the reason, I don't feel as shy as I expect to when Daddy closes the door to our room at the hotel, shutting us in together.

Instead, I feel only relief. It's the first time we've been alone together, without interruption, in what feels like ages. Daddy, though, doesn't look relieved. He looks hungry.

For a second, the old fear fills me. What if he takes too much? What if he doesn't stop? I shove it ruthlessly down.

"I trust you," I say out loud to him, tugging on the collar of my shirt until it's falling down my shoulder. I tip my head, baring my throat, and Daddy's eyes flash scarlet.

"Are you sure? We can wait until—" Daddy hesitates but his fingers are twitching.

"No. *Now*, Daddy. I want to be yours again," I interrupt him, ready now that I've gathered my nerves.

"Oh, Eryn," Daddy purrs, approaching with all the sleek grace of a hunting lion. "You've always been mine."

With a burst of courage I didn't know I had, I grin and say, "Prove it."

He does. With little regard for the fact that this shirt is the only one I own—in my hurry to get to Old York and find out about Levi, I hadn't thought to take anything from Havenwood—Daddy grabs the collar and tears it open. Buttons pop off, flung left and right by the force of it.

Then Daddy winces, shaking his hand, and I can't help but giggle. I snag his hand and drop a kiss to the red mark on his palm. How did he give himself a friction burn on my shirt?

He chuckles. "That'll take some getting used to."

I grin. "I'll be happy to practice as often as you need to, Daddy."

"Little minx," he says, but I can tell he doesn't mind, especially when he shoves my ruined shirt over my shoulders and lets it fall to the floor. He doesn't pick me up—he'd very apologetically explained earlier that he wasn't as strong now as he was used to—but instead he walks me toward the bed, until my knees hit the mattress and I fall onto my back. "Scoot up, sweetheart," he murmurs.

As soon as I do, he crawls onto the mattress, settling between my thighs as soon as I stop moving. He lowers himself down above me, and rather than frighten me, his weight is like a security blanket, chasing away my worries.

He doesn't bite me immediately.

Instead, he takes several moments to trace his fingertips over my face like he's mapping it out, from my forehead down my nose, along my jaw then down my neck, over and over, his fingers soft and warm.

"So pretty," he whispers, then his lips are on mine, stealing my breath from my lungs.

As soon as he pulls away, I miss the contact, trying to chase his mouth with mine with no luck.

"Patience, sweetheart," Levi scolds me, but his eyes are twinkling. He moves lower, running his mouth along my jaw hard enough that I feel his teeth. They don't break the skin, only threaten, and he hums over the pulse in my neck.

My breath catches, and I let my head fall back farther, feeling the cords in my neck tighten as I strain, waiting for the bite.

Just when I start to worry that he's changed his mind, he does it. He sinks his sharp teeth into my skin and starts to suck. My cock goes from half-hard to fully erect and throbbing in no time at all, and I whine, fisting my hands into the sheets as I try to be good and not touch.

Sooner than I expect—surely he got only a mouthful or two?—he slides his teeth from my skin and runs his tongue over the already-healing wound. He lingers well after the pain has faded, and each stroke of his tongue on my flesh sends jolts of pleasure straight to my cock.

"Please, Daddy," I finally blurt out, unable to take it anymore. I thrust my hips upward until they meet a similar hardness between Daddy's thighs, and it's his turn to moan.

"Patience, sweetheart," he murmurs, but there's a fire in his eyes that matches the one burning inside me. He gives my neck a final lick before he slides lower, running his soft, blood-tinged lips down my chest until he reaches a nipple.

He takes it into his mouth, the damp wet heat sending shocks through me. My toes curl and I quiver. "It's too much, Daddy!"

I can't help it. I slide my hand between us and down. I've got it half buried into my waistband before Daddy growls, his hand — weaker than he might be used to but still stronger than mine — grabbing my wrist. He pins it to the bed. I wait for the panic to come — because surely it must, right? — but it doesn't.

I flex my fingers, twisting my arm to test his grip, but it's solid. He holds my gaze like he's analyzing my response, and he must decide I like it, because he doesn't release me. Instead, his smile stretches across his face. It makes me feel like a bunny being stared at by a predator — a wolf on the prowl — and the irony isn't lost on me.

I swallow, and his gaze drops to my neck, his eyes darkening with lust. "Tell me I can take you, sweetheart."

I moan and spread my legs wider in answer, splaying them on either side of his hips. "Please, Daddy. Show me who I belong to." The words come out passionate and strong, and it seems to surprise him. He rocks back on his haunches for a second and slides his hand into his pants. The outline of his hand grabbing his dick and squeezing is obvious.

"Take off your pants," he orders, his voice strained, and I hurry to obey, shucking them in a less-than-graceful movement before I toss them to the floor. Considering the condition he left my shirt in, I doubt I have to worry about a bit of dust. While I'm getting naked, he stretches toward the nightstand to the left of the bed, yanking out one drawer after another before he crows with pleasure. "Knew they'd have it," he says, almost to himself, before he drops a small, sealed bottle of lube right onto my belly.

It bounces and almost rolls off until I grab it. While Daddy works out of his pants, I lift the bottle to my teeth and tear at the plastic. I don't see where it falls once it's off.

"Someone's impatient," Daddy says with a grin, rolling off the bed and standing up so he can let his pants drop.

I nod back as seriously as I can manage, wisely I think, since I don't want him waiting any longer than necessary. "I missed you," I answer, and his expression softens. I take a second to stare at him — something I never felt comfortable doing, before. Now, I want to memorize every part of his body.

I want to know what he looks like with my eyes closed, what he feels like with both my hands tied behind my back. I want to know everything.

I don't know if he realizes I'm staring and pauses to give me time, or if he's just showing off all on his own, but he spreads his arms and tips his head up. I stare, taking in every inch of exposed, pale flesh. He doesn't have freckles the way I'd expect someone with his complexion to have, just miles of porcelain. He has shoulders that are broader than mine and narrow hips, with legs that seem to go on for miles.

I take in all of that in seconds, before my gaze catches on his cock. It's hard and straining and aiming right toward me, and I want it. I prop myself up on my elbows and bend my knees, displaying myself for him in return.

He rumbles out an appreciative sound and drops his hand, crawling onto the bed so he can settle between my thighs again. He cups a hand over each of my knees, urging them apart even farther, until I can feel the strain in my hips. Then, he pushes them up toward my chest.

"Hold them for me, sweetheart," he says, not letting go until I've curled my hands around the back of my thighs, keeping my legs up and apart. I'm fully on display for him now, even more so than I was before, and he doesn't waste any time.

He dives forward, burying his face between my cheeks too quickly for me to prepare for. He goes after my hole like a man possessed, starving for every taste he can get, and he's quickly turned me into a whining, whimpering, writhing mess.

I don't mean to, but suddenly, without any conscious thought from me, my hands are in his hair. As soon as I feel the silken strands weaving through my fingers, I freeze, my heart pounding. I wait for him to scold me, but he doesn't.

Instead, he moans, the sound vibrating against my hole, and he works his tongue inside. Without my hands to hold them up, my thighs start to burn, and I allow them to lower, until my heels are digging into the mattress. Daddy just growls, shoving my hips up a bit higher with his hands, then holds me open with his fingers.

"Can't… Please, Daddy, too much!" I cry, thrashing my head back and forth against the pillow. I need *something* in my hole—his fingers, his dick… Daddy gives me another lick, a long swipe from the bottom of my hole all the way up to my balls, before he releases me to grab the lube.

He opens the lid and pours some onto the fingers of his left hand, working the oily liquid over them to warm it. Then, he lines his index finger up to my hole and starts to press. It sinks in quickly, thanks to the eager way he'd stretched me with his tongue, and it doesn't take long before he's able to add a second.

It pinches, and for a second, the pain has me tensing, but before my dick can deflate Daddy wraps his right hand around it, stroking me in time with his probing fingers.

"So nice and tight around my fingers, sweetheart," he moans. "It's like you were made for me."

"Feels so good, Daddy," I say as I rock my hips, riding his fingers. With each thrust, he takes a moment to stroke over my prostate, sparks of pleasure uncoiling in my belly.

"Such a good boy. Here's three. There you go. You can take it…look so good on my fingers." His gaze is locked on my ass, his eyes dark with lust, and I swear I see fireworks when he scissors open his fingers to stretch me farther. "Almost ready…" he murmurs, and I can't tell if he's speaking to me or himself.

It doesn't matter, because seconds later, he pulls his fingers out. I protest, but then he's lined up his dick, the thick crown stretching my rim even farther, and I relent. "Oh, fuck," he curses, then he's draped himself forward, blanketing me with his body. I try to think if

I've ever heard him swear before but give up as he surges forward, spearing me on his dick.

It's thick and long and perfect. I cry out, arching off the bed, and he curls his hand beneath my neck, practically cradling my head. Doing so pulls my hair painfully but I don't even care.

He starts to rock into me, and I moan, wrapping my legs around his hips as I shift up to meet him. Then Daddy slows for a second, grabbing my hand and pulling it to his chest. His skin is warm.

"Touch me?" he asks, voice hesitant like he thinks I might say no.

Immediately, I obey, relishing the permission to touch him freely. His skin is mostly smooth, but for a dry patch near his right collarbone — and warmer than I remember. Touching him like this gives me more pleasure than I could have anticipated.

I run my hands over his shoulders — the muscles are tight and corded as he strains to keep himself propped up — then down his chest. He likes it when I touch his nipples, I realize. He breathes in quickly, the sound loud in my ears, and thrusts into me even harder. I don't mean to, but the movement has me pinching his nipple harder than I intended.

Apparently, he likes that, too, because he closes the distance between us with a growl and presses his mouth to mine, claiming it in a fiery kiss. Then, he breaks it just to say, "Do that again."

I pinch him again, a bit harder, and widen my eyes at the expression — pure bliss — that crosses his face. "Fuck, baby," he moans. "You're so fucking perfect. Feels so good."

Every time I pinch his nipples, he thrusts harder, sending waves of pleasure coursing through my body, until I almost can't tell what's causing it—the pinches or his dick. Sweat beads on my forehead, and Daddy swoops down, following the salty bead with his tongue.

My dick is so hard it's aching, and I start to whine, so close to coming that I'm worried I'll do it without permission, but then finally, Daddy's hips stutter and he growls in my ear, "Spill for me, sweetheart. Let me see you..."

I'm so close. I just need something else to push me over. Then Daddy, his hips still flush to mine, his dick buried to the root in my ass, wraps his fingers around my neck and squeezes. "Gonna put a collar on this neck, boy. Make sure the whole world knows who you belong to. Carve my name in it and lock it right up..."

It's enough. My dick throbs, pulsing as I shoot my seed between us, coating both of our belly's until we're a damp, sticky mess. "There you go," Daddy murmurs, collapsing over me. He's heavy, but I don't mind. His breathing is ragged in my ear. My own breathing is harsh as well.

"Will you really collar me again?" I finally ask several minutes later, when we've both caught our breath and Daddy has rolled to the side, pulling me over him instead.

He lifts his hand back to my neck, curling his fingers around it but not squeezing. "As soon as we get back home. I promise. Until then..." He seems to be thinking, then he leans down and sucks at the skin below my ear, then near my jaw, the base of my neck...forming a ring of bruises in the shape of a collar.

Heat floods me, and my dick threatens to twitch, but a yawn slips out. Daddy shifts up to kiss the top of my head. "Go to sleep, sweetheart," he tells me, and it doesn't take me long to obey, drifting off into dreams, safe in his arms.

* * * *

Daddy

Careful not to wake my sleeping boy, I sneak off the bed and into the attached ensuite, spinning the warm water on just enough to dampen a towel. I carry it back into the bedroom and carefully wipe the seed off Eryn's belly, then work it between his ass cheeks to clean up the lube.

I hold his cheeks apart for a few seconds longer than I need to, my body hot at the sight of his gaping pink hole. That's my cum dripping out of his pucker, and someday I want to sink a plug inside his ass to keep it from leaking out.

With reluctance, I finish cleaning him up, then pull the sheets and comforter up over his nude body so he'll stay warm. Back in the bathroom, I do a more perfunctory job cleaning my dick and belly before throwing the soiled washrag into the sink.

I turn toward the door before my reflection stops me. I hesitate, then face the mirror. Leaning in, I examine who I see.

I look like...me.

Even without my strength or magic, I still look like me. My horns and wings may be lost, my other form with it...but I hadn't been using it lately anyway, had I? I'd been caught up in my research and papers and books then caught up in Eryn...and, I realize, I'd been happy that way.

I smile at myself before turning away.

If Eryn can love me like this, then maybe my father's punishment wasn't as much of a punishment as he thought it would be.

Chapter Twenty-Four

Princeling
Seven Days Post Blood Storm

"With all due respect," I say, struggling to hide how little respect I actually feel for the man sitting across the desk from me, "it would be inappropriate to funnel any of the city's limited remaining resources into the building of a memorial before we've finished with the search and rescue." Though at this point, we all knew it was more of a recovery effort than rescue, since any survivors that could flee likely already have.

"The citizens need to see that we understand their suffering—" Alric Timmons, the mayor of Old York, has a whining sort of voice that irritates my ears, which may be why I'm so quick to interrupt him.

"The citizens need to see that they have a safe place to sleep at night and access to clean drinking water and sanitary bathrooms. Which one of those items would we be cutting funding from to build this..." —I take a second to skim through his proposal again—"forty-seven-foot high, garnet-studded sandstone pillar?"

"Well, uh…we were hoping… You see, the police force has seen a roughly forty-two percent decrease in personnel—" Mayor Timmons says, puffing out his chest like he thinks that will intimidate me enough to say yes to his ridiculous plan.

"No. Absolutely not. I will *not* allow you to jeopardize the safety of the remaining survivors by hamstringing the only people standing between us and all-out anarchy. Unless you are willing to finance the cost of the memorial out of your own salary, you're wasting my time." I stand and start for the door, holding it open in a pointed gesture for him to leave.

He's shaking with anger, and I know I've just made myself an enemy. Probably, I could have been more diplomatic. Director Graves would have just smiled and talked him in circles, until he left empty handed but somehow thinking it was all his idea in the first place.

I watch his stiff back as he walks away, then sigh, swiping a hand over my face. I can't wait until a new Director is appointed by the higher-ups at the main office and I can step down.

"Command—I mean, Director Aries?" a hesitant voice says, and I force my eyes back open, giving the young agent a forced smile. I don't remember his name, so I glance at the silver badge pinned to his uniform—so crisp and sharp, I know he's only just been bumped up from Rookie.

"Yes, Agent Chance?" I say, struggling not to look at my watch.

"Oh, you know who—the nametag, never mind. Silly," he mutters, then straightens his spine. "I mean, I have a letter for you? It was dropped off, and the messenger said it was urgent?" He holds out a crisp, linen envelope.

Intrigued, I take it. There's a plain red seal on the back, but when I flip it over, I freeze. Anger coils in my belly at the familiar handwriting. At the center of the envelope, in curling script I know too well, is my name. But not the name I go by here.

Aodhan Nualason

Distracted, I mumble an acknowledgment to the agent, then slip back into my office, closing the door firmly behind me. At my desk, I grab my letter opener and angrily slice through the seal. I drag out the paper inside, certain that my mother has sent another invitation — or some other waste of my time.

Instead, the letter has only two words.

Come home.

Then a pendant falls out of the envelope, landing on my desk with a thump that seems too heavy — a brass Celtic knot, inlaid with specks of gold too small to see from a distance.

I'd recognize it anywhere.

It's Ruari's.

Want to see more from this author?
Here's a taster for you to enjoy!

Demon Daddy:
The Changeling's Faerie Prince
KD Ellis

Coming December 2024

Excerpt

Rory/Ruari

I remember her as she was—the blood red berries hanging heavy from her branches, her knots of May ripe for picking. Now, her boughs are heavy and limp, weighed down by shoots blighted with purple cankers. Once-green growth is black, scorched as if by fire.

The May-tree is dying.

Her roots are gnarled, stretching across the dry earth like outstretched arms, pleading for aid that will never come. My faerie guards ignore her, shoving me past with a heavy hand.

How many lovers has she sheltered in her shadow through the endless summer? How many nights has she stood solitary, a lonely guard against the creeping winter? I feel her sorrow. It scrapes along my skin like brambles.

"What ails her?" I ask, craning my head to keep her in sight. The guard behind me—Maric, he goes by, though I remember him as Anik—slaps the side of my head, breaking my gaze.

"Walk," he orders, not deigning to give me answer. Obstinate to the last, I set my jaw and freeze in place. His next shove sends me to my knees in the cracked dirt. "Your stubbornness will bring you only pain, changeling." He spits the word out like a curse, but it falls empty on my ears.

I know what I am—and what I am not.

No longer am I a mere auf, good for nothing but the breaking of skin. I am more…and less—a different sort of monster, thanks to the ill-fated ritual I'd concocted out of madness and daydreams, a gossamer hope that left me too broken to live but too stupid to die.

I flash my sharp teeth and something close to unease flashes across his face, a fleeting expression that sticks in my mind for longer than it lasted. He cannot hear the May-tree's screaming and cannot feel her sorrow, but I'll be damned if I let him ignore me.

"I like pain," I muse aloud, allowing myself to linger in old memories. I hadn't when they'd held me down and broken my body with lashes from the willow tree, river rock and ash, but that was before.

Before the ritual that changed everything, that twisted my body into this new, wretched thing and carved slivers of sanity from my mind. Now, I crave pain. No heroin addict has ever lusted for a needle like I do for a blade.

Again, the faerie bastard looks uneasy, but he grips me by my hair and uses it to shove me forward. The crabgrass snags at my palms, coarse and prickly. I grind my hands into the bite.

"Then crawl, else she sends the hounds."

Ah, the hounds. Once, I'd raced them and lost. Even now, I can feel their hot breath on my neck like mountain fire. The scars have faded, but the memories are fresh, unlocked as they were by a single, careless brush of a faerie prince's hand.

I start to move but slowly. I'm in no hurry to reach the queen's bower. I'm not scared of the pain that waits for me but of the queen's cunning mind, sharper than any blade she could level on my skin.

It takes us hours. Then again, maybe it costs us days. Time means little in this world-outside-the-world. A flower could bloom for a thousand years but a tree sprout up in the length of a yawn. A single night's sleep could send a harper home to a wife long dead and children grown to elders or send a bard back in the flicker of a candle.

The grass turns to cobbles, cold and sweaty with a sticky dew, and the cobbles to a smooth black path of solid pitch. It is hot against my skin, sucking in the heat from the dual suns, and the grass along its border is wrinkled and brown. We must be near the castle, but nothing is familiar. Before, the path was flowers and stone, not this mockery of pavement.

Maric plants one of his boots on my calf, freezing me in place. A voice above me — a guard, I realize as I crane my head up, just far enough to spot the supple leather of his knee-high boots — sounds amused as he says, "What have we here? A bitch returned to its master?"

I bare my teeth in an imitation of a growl then give a little yip. They want me scared, and they want me broken. I am not foolish enough to think that I'll survive what's coming, but I won't give them the satisfaction of cowering now.

Maric grinds his boot, the treads biting into my skin, but I ignore the pain. I've felt pain, lived and breathed it—and once I'd died in it. My body, this farce of what had once been a man, may blossom bruises and bleed like wine, but it will not break by it.

"She's waiting for him."

Maric kicks me into moving, and I let him. Even if I stood up and ran, where would I go? There is nowhere in this blasted realm to hide where Queen Nuala couldn't find me. The earth is her bones, the water her weeping cunt.

Unless I can make it to the unsidhe, who have no cause to love her, I would be back in her clutches by first dawn.

But the Unseelie Court had separated itself from the sidhe, even back when I first touched these lands, still a babe in the Darrig's arms. There are rumors of unsidhe lands—of trees so tall their branches break through the sky, their roots growing mountains and spectral creatures whose voices drive the living to merriment so exquisite they forget to eat, wasting away.

There's no guarantee I could reach them without a map, and even if I did, I have nothing to entreat them with. They have no cause to love me, either. They'd be just as likely to leave me wandering the thorny labyrinth that separates their Court from this one as to lend me aid.

So instead, I crawl. The floor inside the gates turns to soft wood of deepest cherry, still living but sung into shape by tree nymphs and lovingly tended by the fenodyree brownies who care for the castle.

When we reach the stairs, I go to stand, but a hiss from Maric sends me back to my knees again. "You had your chance to walk, worm."

I don't bother arguing. I lumber my way up the stone stairs and try not to let the seed of relief show on my face. It's slow going, taking them on all fours, and every additional second is one I'm spared the queen's presence.

But all good things must eventually end. Soon—far too soon—we reach the queen's white wood door. Her crest is emblazoned in solid starlight at the center, a mockery in its beauty.

The queen's spies must alert her to our presence because her voice calls out before Maric can lift his fist to knock. "Enter." Her voice is deceptively warm, but goosebumps lift on my arms. The door creeks open untouched, even the castle a slave to her bidding.

Maric kicks me, but my body is frozen, my every muscle refusing to move. Eventually, he gives up and grips my hair, tangling my curls around his fist like a leash. The pain as he drags me inside is enough to stir me from my instinctive terror, and by the time he drops me like a sack of potatoes at the side of Queen Nuala's bed, I've gathered the shreds of my strength around me like a shield.

She breaks it quickly.

* * * *

Princeling

The brass Celtic knot sits on my desk like a beacon, urging me to pick it up. Its message is obvious—as clear as the two words my mother had penned in her own hand.

Come home, she'd written, and this is her 'or else'.

She has Ruari. He may have left me all those centuries ago, may have turned into a strange, broken thing, but I know I can't leave him to her less-than-tender mercies. I reach for the pendant.

As soon as I pick it up, it burns me—hot as dragon fire against my hand. With a pained yelp, I cast it back to the desk, cursing as it rolls across the wood. Twisting my wrist, I stare at the red, swollen knot now branded into my palm.

"What devilry is this?" I mutter, shoving back from my desk and away from the cursed thing.

Even as I watch, the scarlet brand fades from my flesh, but the pain remains, throbbing with heat. The door to my office bursts open, a pair of agents nearly tripping over each other in their haste to be the one to enter first.

If there had been an assassin in here, they'd have finished the job and escaped long before the two finished jostling each other. I stare at them with a dry expression, trying to hide the way my heart is still racing in my chest. I can't afford to show weakness.

"Can I help you?" I ask, struggling to keep my voice bland.

"You hollered—" the first agent starts to say.

At the same time, the second blurts out, "We thought you—"

I lift a brow at their stumbling, tangled explanation. "Everything is fine," I finally interrupt, waving a hand toward the door. "I'm sure you have work to do." I let my voice trail off and lift a brow, leaving the second half unsaid. *Find something to do, or I'll assign a job for you.*

"Yes, sir," they say, this time together, and they stumble back out into the hall.

"The door," I call after them, and it's a mess as they both try to close it. Eventually, however, I am safely alone in my office once more. I return my attention to the pendant.

This time, I grab a pen and slip it through metal chain, using it to lift the pendant off the desk. I brace myself for the magic to strike again, but it seems it must be triggered by physical touch.

Nothing happens.

A twist of my wrist sends the pendant swaying, twisting back and forth, until I'm able to get a good look at its once-smooth backing. What had before been pounded brass was replaced with an iron plate, runes carved into its bumpy surface.

No smith or jewelry maker would have used so rough a hand, and no faerie could have handled the iron by choice. This was surely an addition by Ruari, though I have no clue as to his intent.

Is it a message for me? There's a certain irony to it, the way he turned my gift into something I could never touch.

Grabbing the empty envelope, I let the pendant fall back in. I use an obscene amount of tape to seal the toxic metal inside until I can find someone to examine it.

Then, I pick the letter up again.

Come home.

It seems my mother has finally found the one thing that could draw me back to Faerie.

With a heavy heart, I pen my resignation.

About the Author

KD Ellis is a professional cat wrangler by day, and an author by night. She moved from a small town to an even smaller village to live with her husband and wife and their two children. She loves reading—anything with men loving men. She writes queer romance in between working her two jobs and cuddling her pets— all six of them, which confuses the turtle.

KD Ellis loves to hear from readers. You can find her contact information, website details and author profile page at https://www.firstforromance.com/

PUBLISHING

Sign up for our newsletter and find out about all our romance book releases, eBook sales and promotions, sneak peeks and FREE romance books!

www.ingramcontent.com/pod-product-compliance
Lightning Source LLC
Chambersburg PA
CBHW020323260626
47156CB00004B/1352